D0113979

Taylor Before and After

Taylor Before and After

JENNIE ENGLUND

[Imprint]
MAKE YOUR MARK
NEW YORK

[Imprint]
MAKE YOUR MARK

A part of Macmillan Publishing Group, LLC
120 Broadway, New York, NY 10271

 Printed in the United States of America by
LSC Communications, Harrisonburg, Virginia.

Library of Congress Cataloging-in-Publication Data is available.

ISBN 978-1-250-17187-0 (hardcover) / ISBN 978-1-250-17188-7 (ebook)

Our books may be purchased in bulk for promotional, educational,
or business use. Please contact your local bookseller or the
Macmillan Corporate and Premium Sales Department at (800) 221-7945 ext. 5442
or by email at MacmillanSpecialMarkets@macmillan.com.

Book design by Carolyn Bull

Illustrations by Rachel Suggs

Imprint logo designed by Amanda Spielman

First edition, 2020

1 3 5 7 9 10 8 6 4 2

mackids.com

Unzipped pants.
Slouchy socks.
Shirt buttons that pop off at random.
Scratched sunglasses.
The perpetually missing other shoe.
These (and other) wardrobe malfunctions are caused by poor treatment of this book.

For Rees

WINTER

Prompt: On my mind is . . .

WINTER

Prompt: How do you see O'ahu fifty years from now?

I thought Miss Wilson was talking about my eyebrow
when she asked me today
if I'm okay.
I rubbed my finger across it,
rough now where it was once smooth.

WINTER

Prompt: ". . . A movie, a phone conversation, a sunset—tears are words waiting to be written." (Paulo Coelho)

Sunset.

Tears.

"Good work," Miss Wilson said as she bent over my notebook. "You got the prompt down again today."

Tears are words

Waiting to be written.

"Forget about the prompt if you can't think of anything," Miss Wilson added. "Just write words."

I'll write. I'll get it together. I don't want to get in trouble. That would make everything worse. If Miss Wilson calls Dad and tells him I'm not using class time wisely, the Detention Convention will be just the beginning.

Isabelle came back today. Everything's normal again for her. It's all behind her now.

That will never happen for me.

Use time wisely.

Write words.

Sunset.

WINTER

Prompt: What was your first impression of Our Lady of Redemption?

Notebook.

Whiteboard.

Just write words.

Prompt. Erasers. Posters. Wall.

Synonyms for "Said." Web. Shelves.

To Kill a—

Words are tears

Waiting to be written.

Map. Flag. CD player.

Fire exit. Door.

Write words.

First impression at OLR. Doors—big and dark, holding all the unknown inside them.

"That's your building there." Eli pointed to the smaller square—dark doors, flat roof—beyond the pool, the plumeria, the yellow hibiscus.

I turned to wave goodbye to Dad once more, but he was already driving out the gate.

"That's yours?" I asked about the other building—bigger, same dark doors.

Eli nodded. We were only separated by a couple of palms, a sidewalk.

"Yo, Eli!" they called out to him from across campus, skateboards under their arms, shirts half-tucked, shorts low.

Koa.

Just writing out those three letters together is terrible. Horrible. Small word. Great ache.

Tears are words.

Koa Okoto ran over, pushed his hair from his eyes. "We're hanging out at Pipe later."

Back then, I didn't know what Pipe was—the Banzai Pipeline—the famous wave south of Sunset at Ehukai Beach.

"We can't ride yet," Koa said. "But we can watch."

Mind-surfing, they called it, studying the swell, the break, the barrel.

"Why can't you ride it?" I asked. It didn't make sense that this boy—lean, long, strong, tan—who looked like he was born to surf, would rather watch than ride.

"Hey," Koa said. He'd just noticed me.

"Why can't you surf there?" I asked again.

"Respect," Koa said. "You have to earn it. Pipe's gnarly. If you don't get her, she'll swallow you whole, and she might not spit you out."

In the years after that, as Koa and Tate and Macario raided our fridge and tried to thrill me with videos of wipeouts and waves, as Eli bribed me up to the North Shore with haupia pie, I'd learn everything anyone ever could about Pipeline, the most dangerous wave in the world, with a break so hard, it shook the sand. I'd find out about the coral, the curl, the currents, the timing, the takeoff, the lip that can turn even a master to a ghost. But there was really one thing to know. If the perfect wave ever came, it would come to Pipeline. And Koa would be ready for it.

The bell rang.

Koa asked me if I was over in the smaller square, and I told him, "Sixth." Just one word.

Koa nodded, then turned to Eli. "So . . . you in? For Pipe?"

Eli smiled wide. "Yeah, for sure." Ever since we got to O'ahu, since that first day he went out to Canoe's, he was never ever home.

Before starting off toward the bigger doors, Koa told me, "Yo, watch out for the Detention Convention." But he was gone before I could ask what the Detention Convention was.

Eli shifted his backpack to his other shoulder. "Go get it today, Grom," he said to me, then hurried to catch up with Koa.

Behind me, a white car, fancy, glided up against the curb. A girl got out. She was laughing. Sunlight shone on her hair—the shade of toasted macadamias. If I had hair like that, I thought, I'd never wish for anything else. I smoothed out the front of my shorts. The girl and me, we were technically dressed the same. But her shirt hugged her ribs just right. She was on her phone, waving toward the banyan tree, where a group she's left way behind now was smiling, waving back to her.

Write words.

Desks. Computers. Trash can. Clock.

Use time wisely.

Orchid. Window.

Outside, the yellow hibiscus blooms and drops and blooms again, like it always has.

But a mile away, a white lantern hangs over the Okotos' door.

WINTER

Prompt: Dessert.

My favorite dessert is . . .

That perfume. I know it. Square bottle, silver top.

She's late. That's the third time. She's going to get detention now. Her macadamia hair swishes as she slides into the seat in front of me.

That perfume.

How could she say something so mean?

Write words.

Tali flower. Coffee cup. Crates. Folders. Globe.

We were at my house.

Brielle flipped the page of the October issue of *Vogue*, and notes of gardenia, wood, and lilies lifted up between us. We looked at each other, her eyes wide, the thing about the damselfly completely forgotten.

"Oh my God," we squealed.

The picture was square bottle, silver top. White Gardenia Petals.

We rubbed our wrists all over the sticky strip, held them to each other's noses.

"This will complete my life," I told Brielle. "It will literally make my entire life worth living."

We googled it. It was from London. On back order. Sold out after Kate Middleton wore it to her wedding.

Brielle tapped in her dad's credit card number, told me it would ship in January. She didn't mind waiting. She said if there was one thing she knew, it was how to play the long game.

We went back to rubbing our wrists on the strip. "It smells like candy."

"Summer."

"A bouquet of everythi—"

"Please use class time wisely," Miss Wilson said.

At first, I thought she was talking to me. I was staring off into space. But she was actually telling Tae-sung.

Write words. Get it together.

Dessert.

In front of me, Brielle is writing wildly. About what? Crème brûlée at the Waikiki Yacht Club? Her pen doesn't leave the paper, and she doesn't look up. She doesn't look back. All I can see over her shoulder is the same kind of writing I noticed back in September—none of the letters touching each other, all so separate, wide spaces in between. Nothing has changed for her. She just keeps writing. How does anyone have so much to say about dessert?

Buzz's coconut, limes on the side

Li Lu's text: *shes using u*

Dessert

Would I ever stop seeing Koa—low shorts, pushing his hair from his eyes, "Yo . . . ?"

Dessert.

Duke's Hula Pie

Dad told Eli, "Do whatever you want."

How can anyone write anything about dessert?

Dessert is the worst thing on earth.

WINTER

Prompt: War in the Middle East.

I can't focus.

Notebook.

Scissors. Backpacks. Books.

Mobile. Papers. Tape.

Table. Tacks. Hand sanitizer.

Tissue. Light switch.

Clock.

Even Tae-sung is writing about the war. He's writing and writing, like his life has kept happening. His and Henley's, Brielle's, even Isabelle's now.

"It wasn't as bad as everyone says," Brielle is telling Isabelle about detention. But Isabelle isn't listening. She's writing about the war, like we're supposed to be doing. If I were Isabelle, I'd never talk to Brielle again, either, no matter what. They were friends. I saw them hanging out at the mall a couple of times over the summer, also at *The Dark Knight Rises.* Then something happened. Now they hate each other.

Brielle is doing that thing where she's trying to laugh off how Isabelle's ignoring her. "People make a big deal about it, but it was actually kind of fun." She keeps going, even though Isabelle keeps writing. "You can pretty much just do whatever you want in there. Personally, I caught up on BuzzFeed."

But Isabelle is strong. She's stronger than Brielle. After she stays silent, Brielle looks down and shrugs and says, "Whatever." She rolls her eyes and starts writing, too.

Words.

The war in the Middle East. It's a civil war, Mr. Montalvo had said. The people are all fighting each other.

Shes using u.

Li Lu and me, we won't get pie at Buzz's now, coconut, limes on the side. We won't sign up for horseback riding session at Camp Mokuleʻia. We won't make matching vases in ceramics.

Write words.

The war.

Last night, our history homework was to talk with our family about the war. Before, Dad would've loved talking about this. He would have gone on and on about the "conflict," the "crisis," the "social context." "There are two kinds of people," he would have said, "the authority and the opposition," or something like that.

Mom would have told me about the war in a way I could understand—allies, enemies, rebels, power.

But Eli, even if he were around, I couldn't ask him. He doesn't get things like war. He doesn't get anything that doesn't have to do with surfing. I realized that at the Bon Festival. The dancers danced and the lanterns bobbed—pinks and greens, yellows and reds—and the flute and lute and koto plinked on. My hands stuck to the rail. Mascara melted into my eyes. I tried to untangle the mystery of it all—the dancers, the beauty, the past, the pain. Then Eli said that about the swells . . .

Write words.

War.

The *Nightly News* was on, but Dad wasn't really watching it. "The war," he said, sipping his Gordon's sloe gin and tonic and scrolling through *The New York Times*. "It's the few trying to rule the many."

Just like Brielle had told me. "It's just a game."

Dad was tired. He was tired all the time now.

"There's another thing," I said. "We have to write why it matters. To us here in America."

Does anything matter anymore, though? With Koa gone, and Tate gone, and Eli gone, does anything matter now?

Dad said, "What matters to America doesn't always matter to Hawaii."

"Dad, please," I pressed. I didn't want to get detention for not doing the whole assignment. "Why does it matter, though?"

He answered, "What matters to Hawaii doesn't always matter to America."

Then . . . "Oil," he added finally.

One word—*oil*—cannot possibly be the whole reason something matters. Dad was too tired to help me, so I looked up the war myself. And even though I don't really get it, Mr. Montalvo gave me full credit today anyway. I stayed out of detention at least one more day.

Fifteen minutes has turned into a long time to write in here.

One more minute. One more minute of using class time wisely.

Outside, there's a white bird—a tern, I think Mom told me once—in the plumeria tree.

WINTER

Prompt: "You can't connect the dots looking forward; you can only connect them looking backwards." (Steve Jobs) Look back on the entry from September 4. What has changed since then?

Metals and wedges and MAKE IT MAJOR. I had no idea. About Brielle, mostly. The only thing I had any clue about was the trade winds. When they finally came, they changed everything.

The guitar guy had unplugged the amp midtrack, fighting the squall to coil the cable. In an instant, the Volcom House—three noisy stories of surfers and winter girls—behind us went silent. We stopped dancing. Then we booed—all of us—the pros, the semipros, the regular people. We booed wildly, and Pipeline's waves beat and beat against the shore. Palms swayed, their fronds lashing. Flames from the fire cracked and spit, sending sparks in every direction.

I was laughing. The trade winds were all tangled up in my hair.

"You see Koa?" Eli came over and asked me, and I laughed louder and more. Eli was lit up green from the glow stick hanging around his neck. Ocean dripped from his forehead and chin. He wasn't laughing, and that was even funnier.

"Parking lot," Brielle pointed, even though Eli wasn't asking her. By then, me and her were over, but she was still all in my business.

The waves beat, the palms swayed, the fire spit. It was maybe one, only four hours before the sky would light up. I was: white gauze top, peasant, with tassels, and the winds whispered across my bare shoulders.

"You want a lift, Grommet?" Eli asked.

Why was he leaving so early? Because of Stacy. At first, I thought I didn't want to leave yet. Maybe the winds would die down and the band would start up again and we'd all keep dancing. Stacy could force Eli to leave, but she couldn't force me.

Plus, right then I didn't want to leave with Eli. He was in a bad mood, texting obsessively. I could get a ride with someone else.

I looked around, then over at Brielle. She was looking right at me. She'd heard Eli ask if I wanted a lift and was waiting to see if I was going with him, with Eli Harper, OLR senior, surfer, heading to Santa Cruz.

I knew what Brielle was thinking, wishing. It was everything I ever wanted.

"Sure," I said, catching Brielle's eyebrows shoot up.

Me, I was leaving with Eli. And Koa and Tate.

And Brielle Branson, she wished she had my life.

But that, that was before.

FALL

Prompt: Welcome to LA 8! Today, write about your summer break.

Taylor Harper, LA 8

I wrote that on the cover with the Sharpie Miss Wilson passed around.

Miss Wilson is new here. "Every day, the prompt will be up on the whiteboard," she told us. We don't always have to write about it, though. We can write anything. We can just write words."

It's the most beautiful notebook I've ever seen!

Three hundred blank pages, if you write back to back. Mine is green. Brielle's is blue. Henley's and Isabelle's are red. Tae-sung's and Fetua's are purple.

Fetua asked if we can take our notebooks home, and Miss Wilson said no—they're just for school. Then Fetua asked if Miss Wilson will read them, and Miss Wilson said no again—they're just for us. We'll write every day for the first fifteen minutes of class. Tae-sung looked like he literally wanted to die over that.

Three hundred pages. I'm pretty sure by the end of this notebook, something amazing will have happened. Something big. Something that makes this year everything for me, like it is for Eli.

Eli's applying to UC Santa Cruz. He's leaving me behind, here alone, and it will be just me and Mom and Dad. Mom will worry all the time about where I am, and Dad will be on me about my grades, and it will all be completely boring. But at least I'll still have Li Lu.

Or maybe, like Dad says, Eli won't get into UC Santa Cruz. Maybe he'll stay here a little longer.

Before I passed the Sharpie to Brielle, I added my favorite quote: "Fashion is not about looking back. It's always about looking forward." That's from Anna Wintour (*Vogue* editor) (and Queen of Everything) (and hopefully my future boss).

Today is the beginning. It's the start of making my own life happen, one step closer to getting out of here, off this island.

Out of nowhere, Brielle Branson just gave me a brand-new M·A·C Lipglass! For no reason. All My Purple Life, it's called.

"Limited Edition," she whispered. If Miss Wilson hears us, we'll get detention.

My goal in life is to stay out of detention. My other goal is to write for *Vogue*. I already have my whole platform—MAKE IT MAJOR. I describe the look someone has, then MAKE IT MAJOR. It's like this: Today, Miss Wilson is: flowy orange dress . . . South African, maybe, colors, prints, patterns like I've seen from Solange Knowles?

But also, Miss Wilson is: worn-out sandals, beads around her neck. MAKE IT MAJOR means keeping the dress but mixing in some trendy metals, like silver and copper (think long earrings and/or long necklace), wrapping the beads around the wrist, and ditching the sandals for wedges. Now Miss Wilson is MAJOR glam, the whole next level!

I'm going to change the world, one look at a time.

And I'll know I've made my whole life happen when I get it, the Victoria Beckham tote in citrus, $860. That tote is my life goal.

I almost forgot about the prompt! Summer . . . It was . . . the same as it always is here. Hotter, though, because the trade winds never came. They stayed stuck up north. By the end of August, everything was totally, completely still. We were all suffocating to death. The entire island was literally holding its breath.

The good part is that I barely had to keep the sidewalk clean. That's my chore, sweeping up the plumeria petals that blow in from behind us, the ferns that dry and curl, the palm fronds that drop, the hibiscus leaves that usually blow all over all afternoon. This summer, everything was still—even the fire ant scouts that come one at a time to see if it's safe for the rest to follow.

But other than that, it was like every other summer. Just like fall and winter, even. It's palm trees and pineapples and nothing to do.

Any second, though, the trade winds will come, and they'll change everything. At the end of this notebook, after three hundred pages, my life will be completely different.

WINTER

Prompt: Time.

Macario says in Hawaii the wind is time. It is immeasurable. Unstoppable. How can wind be time? It doesn't make sense.

Time.

It's too long.

Two weeks off right in the middle of the school year is too much.

There's nothing to do.

Write words.

"Where's Eli's plate?" Mom asked last night. Her eyes are clouds now. The skin sags down at the corners of her mouth, and her hair has turned into strings.

Dad was staying late at work. Catching up on some grading or something.

"Remember, Mom," I told her, "Eli is . . ." I couldn't get out the rest. I wanted to say the right thing. But I didn't know what it was. And I didn't want to make everything worse.

Mom got a plate. She set it on the table, added silverware and a glass of water. "He'll be hungry," she said. "Eli will, when he comes home."

Does she really think he's coming back and sitting down and eating with us?

At first, I told myself I wouldn't go to the paddle-out. I didn't have the right to, I knew that's what people would think.

But I wanted to see for myself.

So I put on a floppy hat and big glasses and sat under the pink umbrellas at the Royal Hawaiian and watched them—the whites, the pinks, the greens, the Channel Islands, the Firewires and Rustys. At first they were scattered all around, but they came closer and closer together. Girls and guys, kamaʻāina and haole, long-stem daisies between their teeth. Babies draped in maile riding the noses of Billabongs.

Why did they have it on Waikiki? Koa and Tate would've hated that. When the waves came, they didn't even break. "Ankle biters," that's what they would have called them. Instead, the water rolled softly under the circle of paddlers, raising it up and letting it down gently, one family. One living, beating heart.

The splashing started—one, then two, then ten, then twenty paddlers showered the center with spray. They tossed in orchids, ti strands, kukunaokalā leis. The sisters and brahs all rose up and down together, whistling, hugging, holding hands. They beat at their boards—the people who had known Koa and Tate forever, the ones who had met them just before, probably a few who had never met them at all. Pros, keikis, brown skin, white . . . One heart of color, of flowers, of everything happy.

I didn't expect it to be happy. I didn't think everyone would be smiling and splashing. And while the chanting of their names didn't surprise me—KOA, KOA, then TATE, TATE, TATE—the one voice that called out ELI trapped my breath inside my chest. I pulled my hat down, had no idea what everyone would do. They had to all hate him, like Brielle does.

But the other voices joined the one—ELI, ELI—and the heart beat for Eli. Even though he didn't deserve that at all.

The people out there—Eli's other family—they left what they were going through on the beach with their backpacks and bags.

And I don't get it at all, how they were just moving forward like that. I watched from shore where the cabana boys dug like crabs, stabbing umbrellas into the sand, and I thought about Mom and Dad and me, how we—Eli's real family—will never, ever, ever move past this.

WINTER

Prompt: Collective action.

Art. Outlet. Podium. Projector.

Collective action.

Those people at the paddle-out, the ones chanting Eli's name, do they visit him now, in there? Do they write him letters? Or email? Does he have that?

Today, the tern isn't in the plumeria.

Sixty thousand.

That's how many people have died so far in the Middle East. It came on the *Nightly News* after a sex scandal thing and a clip on the Windows upgrade.

Sixty thousand.

Everyone everywhere is just . . . gone.

It's pouring—it hasn't stopped—and the avocado path will be all washed out.

I'll have to take the #5 bus home.

Home.

I haven't taken the bus since it happened. I can barely even drive with Dad.

We had stopped at the Aloha, Dad and me, on the way to school. We pulled up to the pump, and when Dad opened his door, it hit me, the smell of gasoline.

Dad! I tried to cry out to him, to tell him we were going off the road.

Dad! The word just wouldn't come out.

My arms were straight out in front of me, elbows locked, so when the car spun out, I wouldn't jerk forward and slam my head into the headrest again.

"Help!" I cried out.

Dad was prying my hands off the dash. He was telling me it was okay.

It wasn't okay! The gas . . . the glass . . . the window . . .

My eye, my eye, it was warm and . . . wet?

Dad was trying to hold me. Telling me it was okay. Telling me to take a deep breath. But couldn't he see? I couldn't breathe. The seat belt was crushing my chest, and the warm wet trickled down from my eyebrow.

Suddenly, though, there was a loud honk from behind. And I gasped. I remembered. Dad and me, we were at the Aloha. I could breathe. I wasn't bleeding. But I wasn't okay, either.

Dad let go.

"Do we need to get you some help?" he asked carefully.

He was asking about counseling. "No, I'm okay," I told him. I didn't want him to worry about me. He had so much to worry about already.

I looked at myself in the mirror, pushed up my eyelid that droops down from the rough brow. What Eli did will follow me forever. It's written on my face. Brielle is right.

This is who I am now.

FALL

Prompt: Introduce yourself.

Aloha!! Taylor Harper, coming to you live from Our Lady of Obsession here on O'ahu, and today is the second day of All of My Purple Life. Just enough for the right people (Brielle) to notice, but not enough for the wrong person (Sister Anne) to. Besides that, I'm the same as everyone else: polo shirt, khaki shorts.

Last year, to mix things up, I put on the tie, or the skirt, but this year's been way too hot.

Eli's thing is surfing. He's all about Sunset. Everybody has their wave. Koa's is Pipeline. Macario's is Bowls. Tate's is Sandys. Eli's is Sunset—classic, moody, big. Eli's other thing is Koa and Tate and Macario. And his other other thing is Stacy.

Mom's things are us and gardening and taking care of sick people, and Dad's thing is the university. Once we had a bunny named Hopper, who was Eli's thing and my thing together, but mostly Hopper was Eli's.

My thing is fashion, putting looks together. On weekends/Free Dress Days, I put hoop earrings and skinny belts with ruffly skirts and strappy sandals. Because it's Hawaii, we can't wear any of the big fall trends—velvet, turtlenecks, and boots. We wear the same thing in fall that we do in winter. And spring. And summer. (Side note: In *Vogue's* new September issue, there's a next-level pair of Stuart

Weitzman strappy sandal-boots that would totally work. $750. I wish.) But when I get off the island, I'll wear each season. That's definitely going to happen.

Dad and Mom and Eli and me, we live under the monkeypod trees, at the bottom of the Mānoa mountains. People say the trail to the falls is haunted by Huaka'i Pō—old Hawaiian warriors. If you go, wear your Mānoa Falls shoes. And watch out for wild pigs. They eat everything.

Sandy Beach (Sandys) is just three miles away. Also, the Ala Moana mall is pretty great. Li Lu Wen and me, we've been friends since I came here—and we go to Ala Moana all the time. The day we graduate from eighth grade, Li Lu and I are going to Buzz's—the Lanikai one—for steak or maybe scampi, but definitely for the coconut pie. They put little limes on the side, and you squeeze them on yourself! (Side note: Dessert is the.Best.Ever.) At the end of this year, we get to go to Camp Mokule'ia! For two nights! It's up on the North Shore. Li Lu and me, we're going to sign up for the same horseback-riding session.

Other than going to the mall, there's not a ton to do here, pretty much just surfing, if you're into that.

So, I never thought this would happen, but I'm also getting to be really good friends with Brielle Branson. I guess I always thought she had her group. But two days in a row, she's invited me to sit at her lunch table with Noelani and Soo, now that Isabelle's out of the picture.

Last year Isabelle went to Brielle and Sophia Branson's super-exclusive New Year's Eve party. It was all over Instagram—Isabelle and Hailey, who had their own spin on Greek goddess costumes. It was genius.

The theme was "Heaven and Hell," and apparently the caterers and bartenders and DJ were all dressed up like angels. Supposedly, there was a blue room with just one white couch where couples could hook up, and the pool had blue water, and Hayden Jones jumped into it from the roof completely naked, and Brielle and Sophia were the only ones who wore devil costumes. The whole thing ended up costing their parents $17,000, people said, for the fine they got from the Five-0 for violating the noise ordinance and providing alcohol to minors. No one even would have known about any of it if Komo Kalikoma didn't get a dart stuck in his leg and almost bleed to death, so they had to call the ambulance.

Even though it's only September, everyone's already talking about this year's parties, which are pretty much the ONLY thing happening around here. They're mostly talking about THE party, the one at the Bransons' on New Year's Eve. To get into that one, you have to get on the list. And to get on the list, you have to be friends with Brielle or Sophia. Brielle was trying to tell Elau that this New Year's, they're having a Carnivale theme—with aerial dancers, a fortune-teller, and a tattoo artist. I don't know why she was telling Elau. She's never talked to him before.

But this New Year's, I have to go. I have to see it all for myself, exactly what everyone's still talking about till the next time. I'm already planning out my look—feathers and sequins—that's totally my thing.

Amaretto sours. I heard Brielle telling Elau they are going to have those. She said they're way more sophisticated than the cosmos they had at Heaven and Hell.

What in the world are amaretto sours???

WINTER

Prompt: Which celebrity would you like to meet?

Celebrities.

Once, this answer would have been easy: Anna Wintour, Nina García, Marc Jacobs, Angelina Jolie.

But now I don't know. There's vog inside my head, the dark, heavy ash carried over from Kīlauea Volcano on the Big Island. It's darker, heavier than the fog that rolled into Oregon just before winter came. Nothing can clear it away. We have to wait it out.

Dad's yelling won't fix it.

"Come on, Julia! Pull yourself together here!" Dad yelled. He's "been back at the college for two weeks!" What would happen if he just stayed in bed? He "can't just cancel classes!" "Someone around here needs to keep the roof over our heads!" "We all just have to get through this!"

What if we can't, though? What if we don't get through it? What if Dad gives up and leaves us? Would I leave with him? Would he make me? What would happen to Mom?

On weekends, Mom and I used to go to the library or to Foodland or Curry House. We used to buy stalks of birds of paradise from Watanabe Floral, and do laundry, and read the *Honolulu Star-Advertiser*, but the paper hasn't been around since Eli's face was plastered all over the front page. Someone must've canceled the subscription.

There's a little statue on Miss Wilson's desk, the serious kind of Buddha, not the one who's laughing. It is frozen midstep, one arm by its side, the other reaching out, palm forward, like when he's telling someone to stop. That statue wasn't there before. I wonder if Sister Anne knows about it.

Buddha. There's someone I'd like to meet. He would know how I could survive my life.

Does Buddha count as a celebrity?

"Hey, Grom!" Eli was smiling.

I was in seventh grade, and we were waiting by the gate for Dad to pick us up.

Eli punched my leg. I said, "Ow," and punched him back.

"What did the Buddhist say to the hot dog vendor?" he said.

"I don't know. I don't care. What?" I rubbed my leg where Eli punched it.

"Make me one with everything!" Eli was laughing. He was laughing and laughing into the sky.

FALL

Prompt: Looking forward.

Besides the Bransons' party, there are also the ones up North—the famous Volcom House parties, the ones at Ehukai Beach. You can't get into those exactly. They're for the masters—pros and semipros like Koa—the best on all of earth who can charge the deathwish drop. Those parties aren't for regular people. They're for people who aren't afraid of anything. They're for winter fling girls and cool kids like Eli who know people like Koa.

But. The Volcom House parties—the winter ones—they spill out of the three stories, right into the streets and onto the beach, where the regular people can dance around the fire to actual live bands. That's what Eli says. He loves hanging out at those.

Brielle asked me if Eli was going this winter, and I told her for sure, because he's best friends with Koa, and he's always at Sunset—he basically lives there.

And then Brielle asked if I was going. Which I totally am! Mom said I can go IF I go with Eli.

I asked her, not Dad, because Dad always tells Eli he doesn't want him going to the North Shore, that Kamehameha is windy and narrow. "It's not a good road," Dad always says. "People drive too fast" and "There are potholes and chickens all over."

Once, Eli's truck got stuck in the sand. He's gotten tickets, even towed. His truck's been backed into and broken into and even stolen completely when he left the keys inside and the windows down. That's all happened there.

Dad thinks the North Shore is too dangerous, too far, that the current is strong, that the waves are too big, that the water's moody.

Those are the reasons Eli LOVES Sunset.

He tells Dad he's going to Bowls, which is closer, safer. Boring. Mush. But really, Eli goes to Sunset, where the waves are big and blue, green, then white. They rise and fold, Eli rising and folding with them.

He says, "Come on, Grom, stop burping the worm." He tells me he'll take me to Ted's after for donuts. And I say I'll do it for a breakfast burrito AND a mocha, and if we don't leave before ten. And Eli takes me up on it. He's that desperate for an audience.

"Come on, Grom!" he calls out from the water when we get there. "Next wave has your name on it!"

He never gives up.

"No, thanks!" I yell back from shore, my red-nailed toes in the warm white sand, a *Glamour* beside me.

This winter, now that I'm in eighth grade, I am absolutely, definitely, for sure going to the party at Ehukai. That's what I told Brielle.

The part I didn't say is that Stacy better not ruin my chances. She's causing all this drama about Eli not spending time with her, she wants him to work all the time like she does, and she's been completely PARANOID he's going to have a winter fling with some surfer girl from Ecuador or Australia or something.

Stacy's the worst. If she knew one thing about Eli, it's that he's as loyal as it gets.

FALL

Prompt: What does "home" mean to you?

To Mom, "home" means good dirt. To me, "home" means Mom and Dad and Eli.

Before we moved to O'ahu, we lived in Oregon. And before Oregon, we lived in Arizona. We've had a few homes: a little yellow one with a white porch, another one that was near a burrito place, and a cream-colored one with big windows and a cactus in the front.

Dad tells Eli if he would mow the front like he asks him to do, he wouldn't have to pay Lono Lawn Care. But Eli never gets around to it.

Me, I was up for moving to O'ahu. I was in fifth grade when Dad brought up the whole thing, and I mean, who wouldn't want to live in Hawaii? Dad said we'd snorkel all the time—we'd see turtles and trumpet fish. (Side note: He did not say anything about eels.) And we'd go to luaus and eat pulled pork. It sounded delicious. He told me I'd love watching the dancers in their skirts made of grass. That there was a real royal palace on O'ahu, and that pineapples grew up right out of the ground! He said there were submarine rides, too, and whale watching, and island-hopping to black sand beaches.

I was up for it for sure—sundresses in December, sandals in January, the beach! It wasn't like I was leaving a whole group behind. In Oregon, I always just had one friend who had to move after a year or two. First it was Dakota, then Aliyah, then Jade. Maybe in Hawaii, I'd find the group I always dreamed of having.

Eli wasn't the same as me though. He'd had his same one group the whole time. To Eli, "home" means friends. They were going into high school. He was worried about making new friends in a place he didn't know.

I could tell Mom didn't want to move, either. The peonies finally had their first buds in our Oregon yard.

"Come see." Mom patted the ground beside her. Her glove was muddy. Her knees were muddy. Her hair was damp. Torn seed packets lined the row of unturned earth between the yellow house and the soggy lawn.

"It's muddy," I told her.

Mom took off her glove, ran her bare hand through the wet dirt. "It will take them three years to bloom." She closed her eyes. "It's alive." She looked at me. "My second favorite smell in the world. Right after the smell of my kids."

"We should go inside," I told her. "It's too rainy."

"In a minute," Mom said. She touched a muddy finger to her tongue.

"Mom! Gross!" I screeched. Seriously, sometimes she does really weird stuff.

"This is what we are, Taylor," she told me.

The peonies had made it through three winters. The last one was the worst—months and months and months of rain—and Mom had just moved the lavender along the side of the house, out of the shadows. Her friend Valerie from work came over sometimes for coffee, and she liked her day shifts in the recovery unit. If she moved, she told Dad, she'd have to start all over. With peonies. It had taken a long, long, long time to get them to bloom. She'd have to go back to working in the hospital. She'd have to take swing shifts, or maybe even nights, and she'd get stuck in the ER or ICU where all the gossip is.

But Dad told Mom she could use some sun. He promised the O'ahu dirt was rich with minerals from volcanic ash. He said she'd have plumeria! Banana trees! Hibiscus! That we'd hike to a new waterfall every weekend, starting with Mānoa Falls the day we got there. *'Ohana*! Dad told us—that's the Hawaiian word for family. He put his arm around Mom, pulled her close.

"The hard thing is the right thing," she said, even though I saw her dirt-streaked cheek twitching. If it was a good move for the family, she would do it.

Dad said he'd get on the fast track to tenure. To Dad, "home" means his work at the college. This would be just the wind he needed in his sails—the weather, the people, the fresh papaya . . . Paradise! We had a garage sale and moved to O'ahu—"The Gathering Place." We rented a house in Kaimuki.

All on his own that very first day, Eli went out to try surfing. When he came back, I could tell he'd been crying. I could always tell when Eli had been crying. His eyes got red. Puffy. And his skin was all splotchy at the temples. But even after I asked him what happened a thousand times, he wouldn't tell me a single thing.

Finally, last year I found out from Koa what all had happened. Back on that day we first moved here, Eli showed up at Canoe's, without a board, without any skills. Koa lent him his shortboard, and all the guys laughed so hard when Eli crouched waayyy down, his feet wide. They walked around like that, crouching, wide feet, laughing. "Shark bait," they called him. And "beach leech" and "haole."

That first day Eli went to Canoe's, he came back crying—I know he did. But he also came back hooked. The next day, he got his own board—a used Quintara for $125—and went back to Canoe's. He went back again and again and again.

We've lived a lot of places, Eli and me. To Eli, "home" is also ocean.

"You are SUCH a fast writer," Brielle just turned around and told me. She looked at my notebook. "You write SO MUCH. What are you writing about? Are you writing about your brother?"

"Yeah," I told her, "I totally am."

She thinks I'm interesting, I can tell. Also, she followed me on Instagram last night!

WINTER

Prompt: Collections.

What is he doing in there? All those hours inside his cell? Is someone in there with him? Does he ever go outside?

It came yesterday, the thick envelope, blue. CONGRATULATIONS in yellow letters. He got in. How? His GPA was barely a 3.0. Wasn't it? What happens now? Now that he's—

Collections.

Conch. Sunrise. Moonrise. Triton.

'Opihi. Puka. Harp.

"Are you doing *homework*?!" It was October. I set my Pumpkin Spice Latte on the kitchen table, where Eli was typing like his life depended on it. He'd always said, "Who gives a rat's *** about homework?"

The latte was still too hot. I had a cat's tongue, Mrs. Tanaka had told me.

"Nah," Eli said, not looking up from the screen.

I moved behind him so I could see. "What are you doing, then?"

Eli snapped the computer closed. "Writing."

I was obsessed with why he wouldn't let me see.

Thorny oyster. Cowrie. Cone.

Ni'ihau. Shiva. Drupe.

Can he still go? To Santa Cruz? Will they let him, now, after . . . Will they know? Will he be out by then? How long will he be in there? Months? Years? The rest of his life?

Collections.

Eli and Mom have been collecting shells a long time. Mom used to get up early, and Eli could catch the best swells in the morning. They have found cowrie, conch, and even sunrise, which are going for $200 these days if they're perfect and whole, and if the pickers don't rake them up first and sell them off to Honolulu shops.

If you want a good shell here, Eli says, you have to buy it or dive for it yourself. Or you have to get up before the pickers.

My whole Hawaii life, I'd been trying to find a shell that fit in Mom's and Eli's collection. Mom was so happy when Eli came back with a cone, a bubble, a harp. She looked it all over, at every fleck and groove. She studied each suture, the lip. She'd tell Eli, "Good find," and then she'd set it on the kitchen windowsill between urchin, drupe, and thorny oyster.

"Good find," Eli told me.

It was late September last year, at Sandys. He looked over my chipped harp like Mom always did, his long hair dripping ocean on it. "Come on, Grom!" He ran back toward the waves, board under his arm, leash whipping at his calves, leaving me on the shore with a worthless shell in my hand.

FALL

Prompt: Influence.

Miss Wilson said she was in the Peace Corps! That makes sense because of her style. It's definitely not my kind of style. But it's a style, I guess.

Today, she is: long lavender blouse, long orange skirt, and same sandals. MAKE IT MAJOR: Make it a maxi! Tuck in the shirt, pull up the skirt for a high-waisted look, belt with a dark bow.

Miss Wilson taught English, she told us, in Lesotho, where the people wear grass hats and head scarves and blanket shawls in every color.

Maybe I'll join the Peace Corps someday.

Or I'll start up my own charity. I'll travel all over, to India, helping thousands and thousands of poor people, just like Angelina Jolie.

Brielle asked me to sit with her at lunch today! First, we talked about how Kevin Loo called Jasmine Fukasawa "thirsty" on Instagram because she broke up with him and is into Elau Parks now, and then we talked about last night's *Project Runway* episode. The contestants all had to go out in the street and sell stuff to buy their own fabric. And nobody wanted to work with Elena. Her shirts came out really bad. Plus, she had an awful sales pitch. She should have been eliminated. But in the end, Alicia was out.

Honestly, sometimes elimination is just so random.

I asked Brielle why she isn't friends with Isabelle anymore. Brielle shrugged and said it turns out Isabelle isn't as straight-up as she pretends to be.

That was surprising. What I knew about Isabelle was that everyone liked her. She hung out with all kinds of people, not just her bestie, Hailey Iona, not just the volleyball team, either. You'd see her with the Hula Club, with GSA, Brain Bowlers, surfers, even.

Isabelle was brave. She didn't care what people thought. Sometimes she didn't wear makeup to school. She posted more pictures of sunsets than selfies. When rumors went around, like how Hannah Maxwell was getting a nose job, Isabelle was definitely not the person you'd ever trace them back to. If there was one human at all of OLR—middle school and high schools combined—who had no reason to get on anyone's bad side, it was literally Isabelle Winters.

I definitely wanted to know more about it, like what happened, and who said/did what, and if Isabelle's still invited to Carnivale. I couldn't really ask Isabelle about it. Even though she sits by me in language arts, she gives off a vibe that she wants to be left alone. She pretty much shut herself off from everyone.

Brielle asked, "Hey, does your brother still have that girlfriend?"

My lunch was peanut butter and honey on wheat bread that Mom had made, and it was making me die of thirst on the hottest day on Planet Earth.

Technically, Brielle had a green tea smoothie and a salmon roll. But really, she wasn't eating any of it.

"Stacy?" I asked, hiding my dry, sticky mouth with my hand.

"Yeah, I guess that's her," Brielle said. "Are they still together?"

"Yeah, they're still together."

"So, what do you think of her?"

"I think she's paranoid," I said, thinking about asking Brielle for a sip of her green tea smoothie. "She's always thinking Eli's going to have some winter fling with a big-time surfer girl. My dad isn't a fan, either, but my mom likes her fine, I guess."

"Really?" Brielle bit at the straw in her smoothie. She was into it, hearing about my life. I had important stuff to say, stuff that mattered. I thought about telling her I found the perfect twist on my Carnivale outfit—while everyone would be wearing feathers on top, I was picturing a strapless mini with feathers on the bottom—but it seemed too early. I wasn't invited yet, I reminded myself. But I could keep talking about the Stacy stuff.

"Yeah," I said. "My dad thinks she's a 'bad influence' on him—on Eli, I mean—because she's not going to school, and she's older than him, and she's kind of out of control."

"Really?" Brielle leaned forward. "Like, how?"

"For one," I said, "she's always telling Eli how to live his life."

Brielle slid her green tea smoothie toward me and asked, "Like . . . ?"

"Like," I said between amazing sips, "Eli asked Stacy if she wanted to go to Homecoming—I heard him telling Tate about that. But she has to work, and she doesn't want Eli to go without her, so now he can't go, either. So while Stacy works, he's going surfing instead. When I asked if he was going, he said no, that he doesn't have to stuff himself into a suit, that he can catch the last waves at Sandys instead."

"He told you that? Your brother, like, tells you things like that?"

I told her Eli talks to me all the time. How he talks all about surfing. How he'd rather surf than go to Homecoming. How he'd rather surf than do anything.

"What else?" Brielle asked. "About Stacy?"

So, I can't say I loved talking about Stacy. But Brielle was into it, so I told her Stacy's a total partier. That's what Dad thinks. He was losing it about that last night. But I didn't tell Brielle that last part.

"Another C in English. Again." Dad was standing in the kitchen with Eli's progress report when Eli walked in, kicked off his flip-flops.

Eli didn't say anything. But I did hear him kind of snort.

Dad went on. "How?! How is this happening again?"

Eli shrugged.

"You know how to write," Dad said. He told Eli he writes better than half his students at the college. He said, "You could do something with that."

Eli dug through the freezer, took out a frozen pizza. He ripped open the box and stared right at Dad.

"I'm not like you," he said.

FALL

Prompt: Picture Day!

"She's pretty," Brielle said about Stacy today at lunch. She said she stalked her on social media.

"Yeah, kind of, I guess," I said. "If you're into neck tattoos and the whole '40s pinup look."

I didn't want to talk about Stacy. Again.

I wanted to talk about Isabelle, and that whole thing. When was Brielle going to tell me about it? Why was it some random mystery?

Yesterday in language arts, Isabelle turned and looked at me like she was going to say something. Her eyes were soft, and her mouth opened a little, but she bit her lip and turned back around.

"She's pretty," Brielle said again about Stacy. "What is she, size zero?"

I had no idea what size Stacy was. I'd never thought about it. But speaking of looks, it's Free Dress! Picture Day!

Brielle is: slate-gray dress with a black belt, a long silver key necklace, AND those strappy Stuart Weitzmans that JUST came out in *Vogue.* MAKE IT MAJOR: already perfect. Amazing.

I told her I LOVE those Stuart Weitzmans, and she said I can borrow them!!!

Me, I'm: striped maxi, black next-level wedges, and a double chain (the look Rachel Zoe just wore in St. Barth).

"Oh. My. Gosh." Li Lu completely interrupted our whole conversation when she sat herself down at our table. "Are you talking about STACY—Eli's girlfriend? You think she's KIND OF pretty? Um, she's totally MODEL material!"

How long had Li Lu been listening? I swear, she has bionic ears.

Li Lu was: lacy white top with a pointy collar buttoned right up to her neck. She was always interrupting my life, being so dramatic about everything.

Still, it was my job to protect her, right? What could I do? What could I say? She had put me in such an awkward position. Again. And I was trying to think of something—before Brielle did. I just had a feeling the whole thing could go south, and it would all be so unnecessary.

Was it possible to be friends with both Li Lu and Brielle?

Brielle was quicker than I was. She flicked her ponytail, and her drop-down diamonds shivered.

She said to me, but loud enough for Li Lu to hear, "*Who* wears a white top on Picture Day when white tops are our regular *uniform*?"

Li Lu pulled the collar from her neck. She looked at me, got up, and walked away.

I couldn't eat. But the whole thing didn't faze Brielle. Her eyes popped out and she swirled her finger in the "crazy" sign, then whispered to me, "SHE is a wingnut."

WINGNUT! I had never heard that before. It was hilarious!

Li Lu took everything so seriously. But also, she was tough. She'd get over the white top thing. It wasn't that big of a deal.

Brielle and me, we laughed. What everyone said about her wasn't true. That she's mean. That she uses people. Obviously, those people don't know her.

WINTER

Prompt: If you were president, how would you reduce the national debt?

I wish I'd never met her.

Brielle Branson isn't even human. She's a monster. She doesn't have any feelings inside.

"So YOU'RE obviously dieting," she said. She turned around and said that to me, today, right here in language arts.

"No," I spat back. What was she even talking about? It doesn't make sense. Her life is all so perfect, so she obsesses over other people's everything.

Honestly, though, my shorts, they have been a little loose around the waist.

"This is just water weight, that's all." Brielle pressed her hands into her cheekbones.

I hadn't noticed at all till she said that, but I guess her face is a little fuller. She was still the most beautiful girl at school. But she had completely changed her look: long white shirt, loose over low-rise khakis. A blowout had replaced her ponytail. She had probably gotten bored with herself, like she did with everything else.

"I'm just bloated," she added, turning back around.

We were friends. Once. Not so long ago. Brielle gave me the Lipglass and told me her secret and said I could borrow her Stuart Weitzmans.

And now I would trade all that for math homework and pale pink nail polish and malasadas. But it's too late.

And Henley, I was friends with him, too. Maybe there wasn't anyone better for him at the time, either. Sometimes he looks and I look, and when we see each other looking, we both turn away fast, too.

Before winter break, I'd look up from these quick writes and see him resting his chin on his fist, looking at me like I was a crossword answer he couldn't get. And when he caught me staring back, his eyebrows would shoot up, and he'd smile.

Then we started talking. One day into winter break, he had gotten my number from Brielle. She texted me snarky stuff about it, like *i hope u 2 R happy together*, and *backstabber*, and *whatever*, until she finally texted she never really liked him anyway. But by then the game was over, and Brielle and I had already imploded.

Write words.

During break, Henley was in Italy with his family, and all they were doing was waiting in long lines to see naked statues at museums. But the white beans with sage in olive oil were amazing, he had texted. And on the flight over, he'd read *The Art of Simple Food*. It was old-school, he told me. And I remembered. Somehow I remembered that.

One day when the mynah birds were extra loud and woke me up early, I texted him and asked what was outside his window in Lake Como, and he said buses and a bridge and a dirty canal. He asked what was outside my window, and I told him about the birds.

Henley asked me what kind of birds they were, and I told him they'd been brought here from India to eat the mosquitos that had been brought by a ship from Mexico. We learned that in Hawaiian studies. But the birds ended up being more of a pest than the actual bugs. They still are.

I asked Henley if the Italian girls were all dressed up in short skirts and scarves and flat-top sunglasses and statement earrings all the time, like I saw in *Vogue* and *Elle*, and he said he hadn't noticed. He said he was ranking gelato flavors, and when I asked what was number one and he texted back a coffee cup emoji, I was pretty sure I'd found my soul mate.

Do u kno the Aquabats? I asked him. He didn't, so I sent him a link to "Luck Dragon Lady." If he were my soul mate, he would have to know the Aquabats.

After a few minutes, Henley texted back *cool,* which was a huge relief.

Then he sent the word *enchiladas* and picture of a small black cat with yellow eyes, her face in a plate of red sauce.

I wrote: *is that ur cat?*

And he sent back a smiley face.

Henley sent a lot of emojis. He liked gelato. He had a cat and liked old-school cooking.

But a lot of times, Henley seemed sad, like something in him was missing. Was it what he left behind when he came here? His mom? His friends? A girlfriend? He got to go to Italy and stuff like that, but he wrote slowly in his notebook, and he thought a lot about stuff. I wondered if that had to do with him getting kicked out of his old school. For possession, some people were saying. For computer hacking, other people said.

Two days before school started back up, Henley texted that he bought me something from Italy—and we were going to hang out at the mall or the beach or at Starbucks maybe. And then the whole thing happened. So I'll never know what we could have been or even what he brought me.

At one point, in the hall, right when I came back, Henley seemed like he was going to say something to me, but I didn't want to know what it was. I didn't want to be even more wrecked. So I walked right past. I saved myself.

And now, Henley looks at me like Brielle just did. The same way everyone does—everyone here at school, and Koa's mom, and probably Tate's mom, even the checkers at Safeway. They see me the way I see myself. Toxic. The sister of the boy who erased his friends.

FALL

Prompt: You should have seen it . . .

At first, it was just Brielle and me at lunch. The lunchroom was hot—there are STILL no winds—and we were talking about *Survivor*. The new season premieres in nine days, and Miss Teen USA is one of the castaways! I hope she stays in the tribe till the end. It's all about making alliances.

"What do you know about Colin Silva?" Brielle asked out of nowhere. At first, I thought that was random.

"Colin is . . . boring," I told her. He sits in front of me in math and gets an A on every test, every time. He seems too smart to be there, like he could be in precalc, easy, even though he never raises his hand. When Mr. Peterson calls on him, he always has the right answer. And he does all his homework, too. Sometimes before class starts, I try to scribble out the last few answers. Colin doesn't mind. He pushes his homework to the side so I can see. It isn't cheating. It was a few problems, a few times, and Colin let me do it.

"Why?" I asked, correcting myself, telling myself nothing Brielle Branson ever does is random. She always has some kind of agenda. Even about Colin Silva.

"He's a creeper," Brielle said.

I had never thought of Colin as a creeper. Last year, he brought in malasadas for everyone on his birthday. No one does that in middle school anymore. I don't know why not. Anyway, Colin was kind of embarrassed. Probably his mom forced him to do it or something. But it was amazing, having malasadas instead of working on ratios.

"Go ask him if he's ready for the math test," Brielle said.

"There isn't a math test," I told her. Our class had finished the unit last week. I got a B+!!! If I can keep going like this, I'll get a B+ on my report card, and it will be the first B+ I've ever gotten in math and Dad will die of happiness, and maybe I'll get placed in advanced math in high school like Li Lu.

Noelani and Li Lu sat down then, and Brielle said, "Taylor was just going to ask Colin if he's ready for the math test."

"Colin Silva?" Noelani asked.

Curly hair tucked into his collar, Colin was playing his Game Boy, just like he did whenever Mr. Peterson wasn't looking.

"You don't have a test?" Li Lu blurted, her chopsticks hovering over her bento box. "You had the unit test last week, you got a B+."

Li Lu thought she knew my whole life. It was so irritating.

Brielle rolled her eyes. "Oh my god," she told Li Lu. "That's what's *funny* about it. There *isn't* an actual test."

It was starting to sink in, Brielle's agenda.

Brielle stared up at the fluorescent lights. "Everything's fish-kicking boring at this trash school. Doesn't anyone want to have *any* fun?"

"Taylor and I have fun all the time," Li Lu snapped.

I glanced at Brielle. She cradled her face in her hands, popped her eyes like she had a stabbing migraine.

"'Sup?" Soo sat down.

"We're talking about Colin," Brielle said.

"Silva?" Soo asked. "What about him?"

Brielle said, "Taylor's gonna ask him if he's ready for the math test." She paused before adding—to Li Lu, "But actually, there isn't one."

I definitely wasn't going to ask Colin if he was ready for a non-existent math test. That would send him into a complete panic. He'd die of heart failure, for sure. And I'd be responsible for that, no thanks. I was just going to let the whole idea fizzle out/go away.

"Oh my god, hilarious!!!" Soo was ruining that plan.

But then: "Taylor would never do something like that," Li Lu blurted.

It was so embarrassing, Li Lu talking for me like that. Telling everyone what I would or wouldn't do.

"Is that right, Taylor?" Brielle shrugged. "You wouldn't ask Colin about a test?"

When Brielle put it that way, it seemed pretty harmless. Also, Li Lu didn't have to know every single thing about my life before I even lived it.

I got up and walked over to Colin. "Hey," I said.

Soo and Brielle moved to the edge of their seats, grinning. I didn't look at Noelani or Li Lu.

"Hey," Colin said back. He seemed surprised but also really, genuinely happy.

"So . . ." I coiled a strand of my hair around my finger. "Are you ready for the math test?"

Maybe it was the way I said it. Or how behind me, Brielle and Soo were whooping like hyenas. But Colin said, "I know what you're doing, Taylor."

My face flushed. I just could not stop that from happening. Also, my feet were somehow fastened to the floor.

"There isn't a test," Colin went on. "They told you to ask me."

I looked back at the group. Li Lu was looking at me with actual scorn. She got up and tossed her whole bento box in the garbage.

Brielle was face palm, laughing with Soo. Noelani pushed her macaroni to the side.

Without telling Colin anything else, I went back and sat down.

"That was a better show than I even thought it'd be!" Brielle squealed. "A total, serious, epic fail! But A for effort, Taylor Harper!"

I felt kind of sick for a second. At first. Till: "Totes. It was RIDONCULOUS!" Soo snorted up some of her green smoothie.

The snort, the word, it was all pretty funny. Noelani laughed. I laughed.

"Brain freeze!!!"

"Ridonculous!!!"

Colin would live. There wasn't a test. It wasn't that big of a deal.

"Ridarfalous!!!"

"Ridonkadonk!!!"

RIDONKADONK!!!!!!

We all lost it. We were dying, dying, DYING of death!!!

Literally everyone was watching Brielle and Soo and Noelani and me laughing and laughing and laughing wildly. I had seen groups laughing like that, and I'd thought they were so lucky. I had wanted to be laughing with them, wondered what they were laughing about. And now, everyone was watching, and everyone was wanting that, and everyone was wondering.

Colin wasn't looking. He was back on his Game Boy. He was never going to let me see his homework again.

But we had a thing, Brielle and Soo and Noelani and me. We had a word, a joke, a code. We had something only we knew, only we got.

WINTER

Prompt: Lunch.

Lunch.

Lunch is the worst.

It's worse, even, than it is in the halls. Or in the classrooms.

When I walk into the cafeteria, everyone stares. All the loud talking turns into whispers, and everyone points like I can't see them, or maybe they don't care if I can, and they shake their heads at each other—even Colin Silva, who I never even really knew.

Brielle and Soo still have green tea smoothies and sushi for lunch, and sometimes Li Lu sits with them now, too. I watch her throw away the steamed bun, the little orange slice, even the almond cookie her mom packs up for her. I watch her buy green tea smoothies and sushi instead. I wonder if Brielle has told her the secret. Or about the game.

I wish I had a sister to sit with, like Noelani does. Or a team, like Isabelle. Was she trying to warn me, that day in fall in language arts? Was she going to tell me Brielle was bad news?

I wouldn't have listened. I wouldn't have believed her.

So now, I leave Latin just before the very last person leaves class, and I hang out at my locker until the hall is almost completely clear. Then I go into the bathroom and wash my hands for a really long time, then I head over to the lunchroom. By then, the basketball players have slammed their sandwiches and Doritos, and they're in the gym shooting around, and I sit at their table. By myself.

Lunch used to be fun. We would sit there, my group and me, talking and laughing. It was the best part of school.

How has it all changed back for Isabelle? She sits with the volleyball group again—Allie, Ellie, Oliana, Halia. They talk and laugh, like Isabelle's whole life never unraveled. Like Brielle never unraveled it.

Hailey isn't around anymore, though. For a while, people were saying she had mono and was taking online classes from home now. Then everyone forgot about her. I wonder if Isabelle has forgotten about her, too.

Everyone's forgotten about the war. The coverage lasted five seconds. Now CNN and *Nightly News* are all about gun control and background checks and waiting periods and assault weapons and mental health.

Sister Anne asked me, "Are you interested in any school clubs or sports?" when she pulled me out of Latin on that first day back from break. "There's theater, swimming, knitting, the paddle club, Grief Group . . ."

I did appreciate how she just added Grief Group right in there at the end. Like it was just another option along with all the other clubs, even though it was the whole reason she called me in.

"I'm okay," I told her. I had never needed any clubs or sports. I had my family—Mom and Dad and Eli. I had Grammie Stella. Nine hundred one friends on Facebook, 143 Instagram followers.

I had Li Lu.

We used to laugh, and go to Bamboo, and talk out our plan to sign up for the same horseback riding session at Camp Mokule`ia. After that, we'd plan out high school, then the whole rest of our lives.

"It's closed off now," Li Lu said at Waikiki last summer. "There's a guard and a gate and a million dollar fine. And who wants to walk up four thousand steps anyway?"

That was her take on the Haiku Stairs. It's been closed since before I was here, since before she was here, since before we were born, even.

Not a lot of tourists asked us about the Stairs, but when they did, Li Lu shut it down like a boss. That day last summer, we were into making hibiscus flowers from silky material to sell to tourists. They could clip the state flower in their hair or onto their shirt. We burned the edges and hot glued the yellow petals on top of each other, with a deep red center. Then we went to sell them on the beach for $5 each. If we sold them all, we worked out, we'd get $125, and after getting lockets, the friendship kind, from Icing, we'd still have tons left over for manis and mochas and malasadas.

But the tourists didn't want the flower pins. They wanted information. Like how to get to the Haiku Stairs.

"Try Mānoa Falls instead, or Makapu'u Point, or Diamond Head." Li Lu was relentless.

If she'd just told the tourists what they wanted to know, we would have made at least some money. But they left, frustrated, without buying anything. We left, too. We stuffed the fabric flowers into a big pickle jar and went over to Icing anyway to get the "Friends Forever" lockets.

WINTER

Prompt: Have you kept your New Year's resolution?

I didn't make a New Year's resolution.

It was sixteen days after the party at Ehukai. I was hiding in my room, trying to watch *The September Issue* or read *People* or listen to the Aquabats. I was trying to stay out of everybody's way. I was trying to survive.

If Brielle knew that, would she have said what she did? If she knew that I was barely holding it together already?

Or maybe that's why she did say it. "You'll never get past this." Maybe she knew it would ruin my life.

We didn't even have Christmas. Could Brielle even imagine that? Could she fathom getting up in December with no presents, no stocking, no tree?

Dad spent the day on the phone, Eli had gone away, and Mom went to bed.

And if no Christmas, and no more Koa and Tate, and no more best friend, and Eli causing so many problems, and Mom in bed wasn't enough, Brielle couldn't stop herself from making it all so much worse.

If I made a resolution right now, it would be for Brielle's life to be wrecked as bad as mine was because of her. For her to lose everything, like I have. For her to know how it feels.

* * *

"Santa Cruz, huh?" Brielle asked me after school, back in October.

I was standing at my locker, looking at the floor for the "Forever" locket that had just slipped off from around my neck.

People were all talking about who was applying where. Sophia was California. Macario was Oregon.

"UCSC," Brielle said.

"Yeah," I said. "He isn't even applying anywhere else." I picked up the locket and put it back on.

"What's he going to major in?"

I wanted to know that, what he was going to major in. Why didn't I?

I thought I knew everything about Eli. I should have known what his major would be.

"Let's go to your house," I said instead.

Finally, I was going to the Bransons' huge house. In Kahala. With the closet everyone said was ginormous, complete with a velvet ottoman right in the middle and a whole wall just for shoes.

People said there was a movie theater with a popcorn machine. I could see it for myself, the Blue Room, and where Hayden Jones jumped from the roof into the pool.

"You know," Brielle said then, "my house is boring. Let's hang out at yours."

It made me a little panicky, how my house was boring, small.

But before I could try to convince her to pick her house, she said she wanted to tell me something.

FALL

Prompt: Secrets.

Brielle said she wanted to tell me something. But she got all sidetracked by the damselfly first, then by the perfume.

My whole life, all I've ever wanted was a good shell and one perfect friend. Someone I could tell everything to. Who knew everything about me, who I knew everything about, too. Maybe that friend was Brielle. On the walk home, even our steps were in sync.

I told Brielle about the shell, the best one I ever found, a big triton at Shark's Cove. It was perfectly patterned with tan and cream, like someone had spent hours painting it. It was as big as my hand, its scallops perfect and sharp, the grooves smooth, with zero cracks and zero holes and not a single coral attached to it. It must've come from deep, deep down and would have been everything on the sill between the conch and the sunrise. But the spiky little creature was still living inside it, so Eli forced me to put it right back where I found it.

Brielle was fascinated. She liked talking about Eli.

I told her he had been writing something.

"What is it?" she asked.

I told her I had no idea. I hated saying that.

"Well if you don't know something, you should always find out," Brielle said. "You should see for yourself."

"He'll kill us," I said, "if we go in his room. Let's make popcorn and look at *Vogue*. What did you want to tell me?"

"Let's try his computer. Is it here?" Brielle headed toward Eli's room anyway, where towels were scattered all over, and bowls of cereal were left out, and hats and wax and rash guards and leashes were everywhere. I was completely humiliated for him.

"It's probably just something about surfing, definitely about surfing," I said, regretting telling her about Eli's new obsession. I just wanted her to trust me. So she would tell me her secret.

Eli's password was easy. I got it on the fourth try. *Sunset*.

But the document I pulled up, that was different. Random. Weird.

"Perched upon an alien strawberry guava leaf," Brielle read, "one of O'ahu's most striking species is among the last one thousand on the island. This year, the endemic blackline Hawaiian damselfly—*pinapinao* in Hawaiian—fluttered to the top of the endangered list. At one to two inches long, the insect is found only in O'ahu's high rain forest, along its cleanest streams, its rainbow eyes reflecting the hypocrisy of hope and promise."

"This is boring, bugs and guava," Brielle said.

Me, I was stupefied. I didn't know Eli could write like a real encyclopedia. And I wanted to know more about the damselfly—what was happening to it, and why, and why Eli cared about it.

But Brielle opened Eli's dresser drawer.

"Let's get out of here." I shut the laptop and said to Brielle, "This room's a disaster, let's go look at *Vogue*."

A few pages in, notes of gardenia, wood, and lilies lifted up between us. We looked at each other, her eyes wide, the damselfly completely forgotten.

Square bottle, silver top . . . We rubbed our wrists all over the sticky strip, held up our wrists to each other's noses.

"That smells SO good on you."

"Even better on you."

"No, seriously, it was literally, like, MADE for you."

The perfume is from London.

"Candy."

"Summer."

It sold out after Kate Middleton wore it to her wedding. It's on back order. But Brielle is getting it. She'll wait, she said. If there's one thing she's good at, she added, it's at playing the long game.

WINTER

Prompt: Should states be allowed to file bankruptcy?

Bankrupt.

To me, that means beyond any hope.

"Here's the thing I don't get," Dad ripped into Eli on one of the days he was home between Eli getting out on bail and going to the program. Dad didn't get why Eli was driving Koa's Jeep. "So why was it, why were you the one driving?"

Of course Eli didn't answer. He never answered when Dad "talked" to him like this.

Dad always answered for him. This time Dad said: "It's because your truck isn't good enough, right? Because THIS life, the life I'VE GIVEN you, has NEVER been good enough! And where are all the ******* towels?!"

There had been fights like this before. Over Stacy, over surfing—lots of fights about surfing. Eli would be at Sunset, where he wasn't supposed to be, or get home late on a school night, or leave at what Dad thought was a "really bad time."

"I don't get it," Dad always says, "Is it ever enough? You'd rather be out there screwing around than doing anything else, like homework, or helping your mom . . ."

I always look at Mom at this part. She doesn't want to be dragged into it.

"If you put into school a tenth of what you put into surfing," Dad starts . . .

And Eli says he's passing all his classes.

And Dad says, "Passing? 'Passing' is enough for you? Is it being with your friends, is that it, the big draw? That Koa kid, huh? The one who's going to be the 'pro'? He literally walks on water?"

Then Dad goes into how he knows a lot of guys—A LOT of guys—here on the island who just never got over surfing, and now they don't have a life, they don't have a family anymore because they're selfish, they never grew up, and they're never going to. They stay boys forever.

And at the end, Dad tells Eli the same thing: "I just want more of a life for you."

But that's not what Dad said the last time, when Eli stood there in his worn-out Red Hot Chili Peppers T-shirt, that day between bail and the program, not telling Dad why he was driving Koa's Jeep.

This last time, Dad had said, "I wanted more of a life for you."

Wanted. Past tense.

Like along with Koa and Tate, Eli's life was over.

FALL

Prompt: "It's human nature . . . people move on." (Wanda Ortiz, whose husband, Emilio, was killed in the World Trade Center's North Tower on September 11, 2001)

This is the prompt we have every year. In every class. No matter what.

For a long time after the planes crashed, Mom stayed home instead of going to work. That's what Grammie Stella told me. Maybe not everyone moves on. Mom didn't.

I was too little to remember it, but Eli does. He said American flags were everywhere. In the Tanakas' yard, even.

If I were old enough back then, I would have done something. I would have helped. I would have gone on those rescue trips to find people trapped under the broken buildings so they could be with their families again.

Like every September 11, today our teachers made us think and write and talk about it. We had the usual moment of silence, like always, and, like always, Tae-sung got detention for laughing.

Every year on September 11, our teachers and parents and CNN and *Nightly News* and KHON2 all remind us that this is the most tragic event in American history.

The darkest day of our lifetimes, they always say.

WINTER

Prompt: Earth.

Will we get to keep the house? Mom and me, if Dad leaves?

She'll never want to give up the dirt.

At first, it wasn't good, the dirt. For months, she planned, plotted, and picked up starts from the farmer's market. But nothing would grow. It died within days.

"It's not working," I told Mom a few months after we moved in. I think she started working at it our very first morning.

"It just takes time," she told me. Hawaii's growing season is year-round, and once she got the dirt going, her starts and vines would thrive.

Mom worked and worked at the earth. She turned it, worked in nitrogen, checked the drainage.

"Mom, just rent a plot," I told her. "There's a community garden right on Mānoa Road. I saw it. The dirt's good."

"The hard thing is the right thing," she said, tossing a withered kalo start in a heap. "Blight," she said.

Eventually, she asked Mrs. Tanaka, whose cabbage and cucumber tripled next door, for advice. And when Mrs. Tanaka helped her raise the beds, check the soil's pH, then add sulfur, Mom's Mānoa lettuce tripled, her lilliko'i tendrils reaching leeward.

FALL

Prompt: Lockers.

There's going to be food carts! At Carnivale. Funnel cones, and corn dogs, and caramel corn, and cotton candy. Churros and hot pretzels. And everything else you can't find on O'ahu. Sophia already booked them, Brielle told me.

Then, "Hey, Tay," Brielle said in front of everyone, "we should swap locker combinations!"

When you come to OLR, the first thing they tell you is to never, ever swap locker combinations.

But Brielle and me, we did.

Today in Latin, I drew her a masquerade mask with ribbons and the word *Carnivale* written at the top.

The door opened the first time. An empty Diet Coke can fell out, and I crammed it back in with all the other stuff. You would think it would be clean in there, in Brielle Branson's locker, but it was kind of a total mess—peeling wallpaper with pink leopard print, a smudgy mirror with a drooping ribbon and a deep pink smooch in the corner, empty gum packs, fuzzy-topped pens, lots of lip glosses, bangles, and Post-it Notes, some loose pages of math homework, Juicy Couture perfume and a paisley pencil pouch all opened and spilling out on a shelf, a sequined clutch, crusty Bed Head hairspray, an American history book that looked brand-new, a wadded-up twenty-dollar bill, an after-school detention slip from the very first week of school. There was also an iPhone just sitting there, silver and black, with a turquoise case. It wasn't the one she always used. That one had a pink case with a sequined bow.

You wouldn't think a person like Brielle would have a locker like that. Out of control. But whatever. All the stuff in there was so great.

I put the note under a magnet with a sparkly crown that said QUEEN OF EVERYTHING on the inside of the door. And after Latin, I went to my locker to see if Brielle had left me a note, too.

She hadn't.

Yet.

Probably, she couldn't get out of class. Maybe she had a test or something.

She'll leave me something soon, though. I know it.

WINTER

Prompt: Why?

Why didn't the airbag save Koa, like it saved Eli?

Why didn't the seat belt save Tate, like it saved me?

Why WAS Eli driving Koa's Jeep?

Does he ever wonder about us? What we're doing at home? How we're making it? *If* we're making it? Is he sorry about what he's done? About what he's done to us? How because of him, now, any second, the Tanakas could call the Five-0, and somebody else could go away?

I could be all by myself. I could have no one. Eli could take everyone away from me. Dad's voice is pretty much raised all the time now. "This isn't working." "The world just doesn't stop when something bad happens." "It keeps going." And "We need to get through it."

But Eli doesn't have to hear any of it.

Li Lu's parents never fought like this. And Brielle could never, ever have imagined it in a thousand years.

Noelani missed out on everything.

Getting Cut was probably the best thing that ever could've happened to her.

WINTER

Prompt: Caught up.

Macario would be there. At Koa's service. And his aunties and uncles and tutus dressed in white.

And Miss Wilson would go. Mr. Montalvo, all the teachers, Sister Anne.

Stacy would be there, in exactly the wrong thing: tight red dress maybe, off-the-shoulder, choker. And she'd completely forget how she made Eli drive back from Pipeline that night, how she was so sure he'd cheat on her with the line of winter girls just waiting to grab him.

She wouldn't be the only one who didn't fit there. Most of the people who were crying and hugging didn't know Koa at all.

Would Li Lu go? She had a thing about borrowing other people's drama. She lived for it.

Me, I wish I could go. Me, I would like to say goodbye to Koa.

But I can't. I know. It isn't right.

If I even needed a reminder, it was the look on Koa's mom's face, the look she gave me by the papayas in Kokua Market. She must wonder how I'm alive, standing right there by papayas while her son is only ashes. She must hate me for it.

Koa, low shorts, hair in his eyes.

Koa and Tate, they won't ever go to Kokua Market again. They won't eat another papaya, or graduate with the rest of their class, or vote for president, or get married, or have kids or cats or their own front yard.

Koa's mom must be so unforgivably angry at Eli, at me. Tate's mom, too.

I will have to say goodbye to Koa in my own way. I will remember him that first day here at OLR, hair in his face, the first person to say hi to me, warning me about the Detention Convention as he rushed off to get his day over with, so he could catch the lineup at Pipeline.

WINTER

Prompt: How many words is a picture really worth?

From the posts and messages, I could piece together a lot.

There wasn't anything about Koa's actual funeral. But there was information on the wake.

It was at Moanalua Gardens, so many people spilling out from under the big white tent.

The pictures were taken from far away—white lanterns hanging from the Hitachi tree, just like over the Okotos' door.

I remembered when Mrs. Tanaka's brother died, a white lantern hung at their door, too. Mrs. Tanaka said it was made from washi paper, fiber boiled out of shrubs, the same used to fold origami.

What would Koa have thought of all the white? White flowers were everywhere, not ginger ones, like I thought there'd be. Koa's family was all dressed in black, juzu beads and white envelopes in their hands. Those envelopes were filled up with money for the Okotos. But that money wouldn't bring back Koa.

Koa Okoto would never catch the perfect wave at Pipeline.

He had been cremated. Turned from a human being into char that could have once been anything. That's where the pictures end, where his life ended. I couldn't find out what happened to him, to the ashes he had become. Maybe nothing yet. Maybe the Okotos are still holding on to him.

Sophia was in a lot of the pictures. She was: black dress, knee length, flared hem, scoop neck, probably Stella McCartney, hair in a side part, swept back.

Brielle was: black wraparound dress, the kind Grammie Stella told me makes her look twenty pounds lighter but definitely not the kind I'd think of Brielle wearing.

I couldn't stop myself. I clicked on her FB page. I told myself to be ready for the happy, beautiful Bransons, all four of them together, shopping in Sydney, hiking the Outback, snorkeling the Gold Coast, cozying up with kangaroos.

But there was nothing about that. The last thing Brielle had put up was from December 10—a repost: "The prettiest smiles hide the deepest secrets."

That was random, even for Brielle.

Sophia didn't have any Aussie pics, either. Her last post was December 10, too—a selfie at Sandys, her knees pulled up to her chest, no smile. Blue filter.

FALL

Prompt: What do the candidates for governor have in common?

If there's one thing the candidates have in common, it's how easy it is for them to fail. One fail, and they're over. Out forever. For sure. Their past, their policy, their parents' nationalities, their hair, the affair their assistant's husband had—everyone's destroyed till there's no one left.

Miss Teen USA got voted off *Survivor*. She only lasted three episodes. At first, she had made a good alliance with Malcolm. But at Tribal Council, he was the one who threw her under the bus and voted her out. FOR NO REASON. And they let Russell stay. They kept the total bully.

This morning, I was looking everywhere for my math homework, and Brielle came up to my locker and asked what I was doing after school.

I told her I didn't have plans yet. And she said we could hang out.

Out of nowhere, Li Lu appeared. "Tay, seriously," she spluttered, "did you forget we were going to watch *Gossip Girl* at my house after school . . . ?"

Gossip Girl. It was so seventh grade. Okay, we had talked about maybe watching it, not for sure. And we always did that stuff.

And Li Lu said, "Whatever," and stormed off to honors algebra.

"Whatever." Brielle said it the way Li Lu did. Then, "So, your house, then? Will Eli be there?"

Eli was never home after school. He was always at Sunset, or hanging out at Tate's or Koa's, or working, which I was pretty sure he was doing later. That's what he told Dad when Dad told him to mow the lawn.

And that reminded me of Dad. He was going to bust an artery if I forgot my math. I could just hear him: "There are two kinds of people in the world, Taylor—people who keep track of their math homework . . ." I started looking for it again from the top, told Brielle that Eli would be working.

"Where does he work?" she asked, and I told her the board shop.

"Which one?"

The bell rang. I was trying to think if my math could be in my Latin binder maybe? "Which one what?"

"Which board shop?"

"Dave's."

I opened up my Latin binder and flipped through all the loose pages. The math was right there—thank you, mullet baby Jesus. The last thing I can deal with right now is Dad going off the deep end and our whole family falling apart.

Everybody was on me already—Li Lu more than anyone. She keeps making me choose between Brielle and her. It's getting so annoying.

WINTER

Prompt: If . . .

Sophia's blue filter. What does it mean, her selfie at Sandys?

And Brielle? "The prettiest smiles hide the deepest secrets." Today, she is writing and writing. She hasn't looked at her phone even once.

If . . .

If Dad finds out, he's going ~~to kill me.~~

Or

If I hadn't skipped school yesterday, I wouldn't have had detention today.

There is nothing even kind of *Breakfast Club*–y about in-school here at Our Lady of Detention. It is an all-out lockdown, with no life-changing relationships, no solidarity against a common enemy, no essay, even. It's a room with no posters, no plants, no map, no globe. There's just a clock that's rigged to move five times slower than normal, a slice of glass that might be technically called a "window," and the Detention Convention himself.

The Detention Convention never smiles. He calls you by your last name, and if you do anything—ANYTHING—even kind of wrong, like say one word, or someone texts you or something, he gives you another detention. People say the pink pad is a permanent part of his hand.

The worst part (other than the Detention Convention and sitting in there at the crack of dawn) is that you don't do anything. Literally.

And that . . . that is honestly awful.

We sat for a whole entire hour, watching the clock: Myla Marin, who had too many tardies, Ula West, who "talked excessively," and Riley Watanabe, who dropped an f-bomb in science when he spilled hydrochloric acid on his new Nikes. But Li Lu wasn't right about the ice heads.

A whole hour of nothing. It definitely wasn't worth it, wandering around the Ala Moana mall yesterday by myself. Cinnabon didn't even taste as good as it used to.

"Going to school is your job," Dad would tell me. If he found out, and if I had to give him a reason—I just needed a break.

He would say he doesn't get a break. That he's been back at the college for three weeks already. Then, "There are two kinds of people in the world, Taylor: responsible ones who do their jobs and those who take breaks."

Responsible people. Ones with a kuleana.

Even now, Dad still hasn't asked me.

And something like this would just remind him.

And if he asks me, I honestly don't know the answer. I've asked myself a million times.

Why, why, why, why

Why was Eli driving Koa's Jeep?

If

If he hadn't, would our lives have stayed normal?

WINTER

Prompt: Compare/contrast.

Tate's memorial was different.

There were more pictures. People throwing loose shakas, peace signs, arms around each other's backs.

This was Tate's mom's group: black vests, black tanks, black tees ("No man is an island").

Tate's mom was: green sundress that tied on the side, her hair in strings, like Mom's is now. On each side of her were older versions of Tate—his real brothers—holding her up near a vase of handpicked hibiscus.

The memorial was at his mom's apartment in Wahiawa, where all the pawn shops and check-cashing places are.

Stacks and stacks of Costco muffins piled up high in the kitchen—boxes wrapped in plastic that Costco had probably donated. There were all kinds of different dishes on the tables, stuff people had brought. And there were beer bottles everywhere.

This time Macario, the Wolf Pack, Da Hui even, the guys from Ke Nui Road all huddled together on the little porch. They had red cups, cans of Pabst and Red Bull, smokes. Gabe had a plate of barbecued chicken.

They seemed happy. Like Tate would have wanted them to be.

Me, maybe I could have gone to that. They might not have judged me. I could have said goodbye for Eli and for me.

"Goodbye, Tate," I whispered to the last picture: shirt off, hat backward, golden retriever smiling beside him.

FALL

Prompt:* "When you get caught in the impact zone, you need to get right back up, because you never know what's over the next wave . . . Anything is possible." *(Bethany Hamilton,* Soul Surfer*)

The next wave.

That's what Eli lives for.

He balances on his Anderson, dragging his fingers in the water behind him. He gets in the lineup, slices through channels, weaves in and out of the guys from Ke Nui Road.

"Come on, Grom!" he yells to me when he washes up on shore again. "Next wave has your name on it!" He says I could be the next Carissa Moore.

"Not my thing!" I yell back.

Surfing seems cold. Hard. Dangerous. There are currents and riptides. You can get locked in. Or if you get pulled into a closeout, it's all over, forever. And there are creatures out there. EELS. Sea turtles, jellyfish, tiger sharks, even. In the beginning, Sunset was called Paumalu, which means "taken by surprise," because forever ago a hunter stole too many octopuses, even though an old chief told her not to, so a shark bit off her legs.

Sunset's still a surprise. Each swell changes the whole lineup, Eli says. One day he goes left then right then left, and the next time, he goes right then left then right. You just never know.

That's what Eli loves about Sunset.

Some people say it's an old man's wave. That you have to really know it to ride it. And even though Eli's had some wicked wipeouts from there—stitches, staph, scrapes, stings, and the shoulder I'm not even going to write about—he has Sunset as wired as anyone possibly could. Eli leaves Pipeline to the guys who don't mind waiting and waiting and waiting for a wave. He doesn't want to wait. He wants to surf. So he carves out of Sunset's barrels.

"What do you even *like* about surfing so much?" I always ask him.

And he tells me that out there, it's only about the water. The moment. About not thinking anything. About "being with the wave."

Which to me seems completely boring. Not to mention hard. And dangerous.

If Eli wants to split open his forehead, get reef rash all down his side, stub the crap out of his toes, rip his arm out of its socket while he's trying to catch the Big One, that's on him.

WINTER

Prompt: "If you can't fly then run, if you can't run then walk, if you can't walk then crawl, but whatever you do, you have to keep moving forward." (Dr. Martin Luther King Jr.)

This is all he is now, I told myself about that picture of Tate—hat backward, golden retriever—*This is all he'll ever be.*

The picture may stay in my mind forever. It's the saddest, saddest picture in the world.

Keep moving.

Keep moving forward.

"Hey, John," I can almost hear Tate saying. He was always nice to Dad.

"How are you doing today, Julia?" he'd ask Mom when he boxed her up at Costco.

Move forward.

If I can remember Tate living, I tell myself, maybe I won't think about him being gone.

WINTER

Prompt: How did you meet your first friend?

Keep writing!

That's the note Miss Wilson wrote to me. It's on a Post-it, has a star at the bottom. I put it right inside the back cover of this notebook. When I get to the end of all these pages, the note with the star will be there. I'll know I made it.

Keep writing.

Move forward.

After all this time, I can't believe Miss Wilson isn't *dying* to know what Brielle and Isabelle, Henley, Elau, Tae-sung, and me are all writing about our lives. I can't believe she doesn't read these.

Isabelle's writing and writing and writing. Maybe she's writing about Hailey. Maybe she hasn't forgotten her. Maybe she misses her. Maybe she's sad.

Words are tears.

"Forever." That was my half of the lockets Li Lu and I bought after we made all those fabric flowers. But I'll bet anything Li Lu doesn't have the "Friends" part anymore. That pretty much sums things up now.

But before that, Dad got the job at the college, so we moved. "You can make new friends on O'ahu." That's what Dad had told me.

All I ever wanted was one friend, one good friend who knew

everything about me, who I knew everything about, who I could tell anything, and she could tell me, too.

I met Li Lu that first day when Mr. Hayes picked her to give me a tour of the school.

"Just make sure you watch out for the Detention Convention," she said right away.

It was the second time I'd heard that, after Koa had told me, too, and I was completely and immediately struck with fear.

"What is that?" I asked.

"It's detention," she said. "The Detention Convention, the teacher, he's worse than all the people in there, all the ice heads combined. If you say one word or get there one minute late or even move, you get another detention. They say the pink pad is permanently attached to his hand."

"What do they do in there?"

"Nothing." Li Lu's tongue pushed against her crooked teeth. "You literally do nothing. For a whole hour, you sit in total, complete silence. With all the ice heads staring at you."

It sounded horrible—like it would completely scar you for the rest of your life—and I told myself I was never, ever getting sent there.

Inside the church, Li Lu pointed out the carving of the Sixth Station of the Cross, "Veronica wipes the face of Jesus," and showed me that the face on the cloth didn't look like Jesus at all. It was a baby with a mullet—long hair in back, super short bangs—and Li Lu and I covered our giggles with our hands as we stood before the carving.

Back then, before her contacts and braces, Li Lu was: glasses, front teeth all crooked, hummingbird hands.

After that tour, we had lunch together. And again every day after, and all of the next year, too, except the time she blew up at me for "ignoring" her, for being better friends with Jasmine Fukasawa than with her.

But we got over that pretty quick. After a week, Li Lu just said, "Seriously, this is pointless." She invited me to Leonard's Bakery after school, and we stuffed ourselves with malasadas, the cinnamon-sugar snowing down on our white blouses, between the pleats of our skirts.

Li Lu Wen was the best friend I ever had.

I totally and completely miss her.

FALL

Prompt: Sabotage.

Brielle didn't make it over to my house. She forgot she had "a ton of stuff to do."

But then, later that night, Eli said he saw my "rich friend, What's-Her-Nuts," at his shop. "Just hanging out," she'd told him.

What would Brielle be doing on Kūhiō, down by all the hotels? That doesn't seem like her thing.

I asked Eli who she was hanging out with.

"No one," he said. Apparently, Brielle was all by herself.

I wish I had parents like that, who would let me hang out on Kūhiō instead of Dad constantly panicking I'm going to get robbed or kidnapped by ice heads.

Brielle's lucky. Does she know? She goes anywhere she wants, and no one tells her she's going to get robbed or kidnapped, or that she already went out that week, or to be home by dinnertime, or that that road is bad, or doesn't she have homework.

She has total and complete freedom.

We're planning on doing something again, soon, Brielle and me. Even though Li Lu is trying to thwart our whole lives. She just can't cope when I'm friends with someone else. It happened in sixth grade with Jasmine Fukasawa. Li Lu thinks I can't be friends with two people at once. That I'm better friends with the other friend. That I "ignore" her.

At lunch, when Brielle asked if I wanted to hang out at the mall or something, Li Lu started right in on me: "This happened LAST TIME. I thought we were going to . . ."

And Brielle just got up and left.

Seriously. Li Lu's drama is getting so annoying.

WINTER

Prompt: Write about a pet you've had or wanted to have.

Before we moved here to O'ahu, Eli kept saying he wanted a cat.

Every day, all day long, he asked Mom and Dad if he could get one. He would pay for its food, he promised. He would take care of it, too.

"There are wild cats all over the island," Dad kept telling him. "When we get there, just put out some food and they'll come."

But Eli wanted his own.

Dad told him maybe when we got to O'ahu. But then, "A cat is a big responsibility," he said when the plane landed, when Eli asked again.

Dad didn't think Eli was ready. Even though he was going to start high school.

Eventually, I started begging, too. I don't know if it's because I actually wanted a cat, or because I just wanted Eli to have it. But I started in on Dad and Mom, too. And after our begging for a cat wasn't working, we started in on getting a bunny. We could name him Hopper and hold him in our laps.

One super humid afternoon, Mom gave in and took Eli and me—"Just to LOOK"—to Petco in Pearl City. And there were all kinds of bunnies—white, brown, big, small . . . Eli wanted to buy one right then. He had his own money, and he kept asking, and Mom always had a hard time not giving in to him. Finally, she said that if he showed he could be responsible by unloading the dishwasher every day and putting away his laundry and making his bed without being asked until the day before school started, he could get one.

I never thought it would happen. Usually, Mom asked Eli twenty-five times to unload the dishwasher and put away his laundry and make his bed, and he still never did it.

But Eli ended up unloading the dishwasher and putting away his laundry and making his bed. Every day. He even mowed the lawn. Dad told Mom he'd never seen Eli work so hard for anything in his life. (He said that again when Eli saved up the half Dad matched to buy his truck, the only two times Dad said Eli ever worked hard.)

And, the day before school started, Mom and Eli and I went back to Petco, and Eli picked out his bunny—brown and white, medium-sized, with round, black eyes and long, floppy ears. I wanted my own bunny, too, but Mom said one was enough to start with. Eli named that bunny Hopper.

Dad warned him: "Don't forget to check the latch on his cage. If that rabbit gets out, he'll be lost in the Mānoa mountains in no time." The wild pigs would find him and eat him in five seconds flat.

School had started, and every day Eli got up early and fed Hopper and changed his water and slipped a little of Mom's Mānoa lettuce into his cage. And after school or after surfing, Eli came right home and got Hopper out and held him on the grass there for hours. He never let me hold that bunny, though.

"Not yet," he kept saying. He didn't think I was ready.

"Did you check the latch?" Dad asked every night at dinner.

And every time, Eli said he had. Sometimes he even snuck out of bed so he could triple-check.

Me, I wanted to hold Hopper so bad, but Eli wouldn't let me, not even for a minute. He kept saying Hopper was skittish. Hopper didn't look skittish, though. He lay right in Eli's lap, and let Eli pet him between his long, floppy ears. When I told on Eli, Mom said that was probably true about Hopper's being skittish. No one was on my side.

One day, when Eli had to stay after school to finish the book report he didn't turn in, I wrestled Hopper out of his cage and held him in my lap with my legs crossed, exactly like Eli always did, but Hopper wriggled around wildly and I had to sort of pin him down. He didn't like that. He twisted and kicked and clawed at me, and I was so surprised I let go.

That's when Hopper ran across the whole backyard, straight into the Mānoa mountains. I chased him as fast as I could, but that bunny was faster.

I cried when I told Eli, but Eli cried more. His cry was different. Like, out of pain. I've only heard Eli cry like that one other time. "The pigs got him!" he sobbed.

That night at dinner, Dad asked Eli if he checked Hopper's latch.

I froze in my chair. I knew I should say I let Hopper get away. But I didn't.

Eli's chin dropped down to his chest. Mom asked, "Did something happen?" And Eli said Hopper got out.

Dad had both hands on the table. Part of me hoped he wouldn't find out it was my fault. And another part hoped he would. I felt awful. I could have said it was me who lost Hopper, but I didn't. The longer I sat there not saying anything, the worse I felt, and the less chance I had of getting any words out.

Dad said to Eli: "He's gone? After only three weeks? Like I told you, pets are a big responsibility." Dad said there were two kinds of people in the world—those who are ready for responsibility, kuleana, and those who aren't.

Eli was ready. He loved that bunny. I saw it when he held him, when he fed him, when he found out Hopper was gone forever. But he covered for me. He covers for people. It's who he is.

FALL

Prompt: Don't write anything yet.
Close your eyes until the teacher says "Begin writing."
Then write. What did you notice?

I LOVE writing.

That's what I noticed.

And another thing. Miss Wilson made us sit waaaayyyyyy too long. It was awful, having to sit and do nothing. I'd rather do anything than nothing.

I can say for sure that it killed Brielle, too. She was sighing, looking all around. I could almost hear her: *This is SO boring.*

Brielle's always doing fifty things at once. Almost every day, Miss Wilson says if she sees her texting in class, she's going to have to leave her phone in language arts till after school. Brielle always says she isn't texting, which is kind of true. She's actually scrolling through topshop.com or Instagram, and once, over her shoulder, I saw her swiping and swiping through pictures of super-skinny girls.

Sometimes Brielle is sneaky enough to keep her phone. But sometimes she's not, and today is one of those days. Lucky for her, she has a backup in her locker.

Some people probably liked it, sitting and not writing. Someone like Tae-sung, who can't focus on anything and hates writing, and gets Ds on all his essays, and sometimes even Fs. Miss Wilson always tells him to put away the paper clip, to use class time wisely.

Henley doesn't write much, either. After the whole fifteen minutes, there's only about five lines. He writes, then stops, then writes again. He writes in mechanical pencil, and when he pushes it too hard on his notebook, the lead breaks off, and he tries to put it back in till Miss Wilson tells him to keep writing.

Our notebooks were right there. Our pens, too.

I wanted to write. I was DYING to write. I had something to write about.

She told me, Brielle did. She said she'd never told anyone.

Last year, she dressed up in green corduroy overalls and a hipster beanie and posted a video of herself crushing on Chance Cameron. Chance was a sophomore. He wasn't popular or anything. He was on the swim team and worked at Hula Dog. Apparently, Chance found out about the video. He took Brielle to Sandys and kissed her on the lifeguard stand under the stars—

which would've been dreamy if his lips weren't bleeding from being so chapped.

"Did you go out again?" I asked. "You and Chance?" I wanted to know everything. I was already in on something so big.

Brielle said it was just the one time.

"Did you talk?" I asked. "After? Were you . . . together?"

"He's boring," Brielle said, then, "Have you kissed anyone?"

I thought about telling her how I liked Kevin Loo in sixth grade, my first year here. But his tight polo shirts seemed so insignificant to the big thing she had done. So I just said not yet.

We made smoothies, and hung out in my room, and put together looks, and talked about how hot Henley Hollingsworth is, and how

Brielle heard that Koa has one last chance. She heard Sophia saying if he "crosses the line again," his parents are sending him to military school in Virginia.

Me, I thought Koa had everything all worked out. He's trying to make it to the WSL Tour. He's already a junior pro. Eli says Koa is up riding Pipeline before anyone else's footprints are in the sand.

I thought Koa was making his life happen.

"Really?" I said. "Koa doesn't seem messed up. He seems like he has it all together."

"Those are exactly the people you have to watch out for," Brielle said. "NOBODY has it all together."

WINTER

***Prompt: How does Scout change in* To Kill a Mockingbird?**

Scout.

I can't honestly remember how she was before.

I used to be able to remember anything, without even trying. I was getting an A in Latin, because memorizing was no big deal. Now, I can't keep a single thought in my brain. Numbers make no sense at all. I'm pretty sure my brain got damaged by the airbag, even though the doctor said I'm okay.

I had to go see Sister Anne again.

It wasn't Miss Wilson who referred me. I've been using class time wisely every single day. It was Mrs. Whipple. I'm failing math. And to make up for the F I got on the test, Sister Anne assigned me two weeks of afternoon sessions at the math tutoring center.

F, D, C, B, A.

We're all reduced to a single letter here. It's all we are.

It's been almost month since Mom has picked up a pen. Or a toothbrush. Yesterday, I heard Dad telling her, "Julia, you need to get it together here. Your sick leave is running out. You need to get up and get yourself dressed and TRY to go back to work, because this isn't helping anybody. We all need to get through this."

Dad, MLK—everyone thinks it's possible to get through it, to move forward.

If I knew for sure how long it would take, if I had an end date when this would all be behind me, I might be able to get through it, to move forward. But there's no end date, no way to know how long it's going to take.

Back in Oregon, I had my first babysitting gig. The Greens' mom had to take one of the kids to the dentist, and she asked if I could watch the others for two hours. I was excited. It was my first job, and I was going to make real money. For those two hours, the kids were bad. They kept saying, "Our mom lets us ride the skateboard inside," when I knew she really didn't. They said, "We don't have to do what you say" and "We're going to tell our mom you were mean." It was rough, keeping those kids in one piece, keeping the house in one piece, too. But I told myself over and over and over that I could do it. Because their mom would come back after the dentist.

I never babysat the Greens again. We moved pretty soon after that. But it stuck with me, how I got myself through two hours because I knew it would be two hours.

This isn't like that.

Mom only eats, I'm pretty sure, when I come home from school and make her something, and even that's only a bite or two of toast. Yesterday, I tried making the macadamia cookies she's always loved, but they turned out thin and flat, and Dad yelled at me for making a mess in the kitchen, then went to his office to grade.

There was a time, only a month ago, when we sat—all four of us together—in the rattan chairs around the table, with something in the middle, like teriyaki chicken and rice and little Mānoa lettuce heads straight out of Mom's garden that we each got our own of.

At lunch today, the table near Brielle's group was open, and I sat there with my baggie of Cheerios. Li Lu was eating salmon roll—you could tell by the pink slab on top. Li Lu always hated salmon, but she was telling everyone how amazing it was. Do people really change just like that? Is it possible to hate salmon one day and the next it's your new fave? Did Scout change like that?

I watched Brielle and Li Lu and Soo talking to each other about going to the beach or to P. F. Chang's after school, and how much fun they had at the talent show they had all already gone to together, and about how they saw Henley with Jasmine Fukasawa at the mall. Brielle said that part extra loud and looked right at me.

Henley was with Jasmine? I thought she was into Elau Parks? After she was with Kevin Loo. She obviously moved on fast.

Henley moved on fast, too. He's over me. I wasn't anything to him.

Then Brielle said, "This is boring, let's go." And they all got up to talk trash in the courtyard.

Li Lu looked down at me for a second, her shoulders slumping a little—I saw it—but Brielle grabbed her arm and told her, "Come on."

And I was back to sitting by myself, wishing it was me with Henley, sharing a Cinnabon, extra frosting.

WINTER

Prompt: Describe an old photo.

Before Dad went around the house and took down all the family photos, I grabbed one off the shelf from between *Freakonomics* and *The Tipping Point* and stuck it in my nightstand drawer.

The photo was taken when I was about five and missing a few front teeth. We were at Evergreen Christmas Tree Farm; Mom thought it would be fun to go out in the snow and cut down our own tree instead of buying one from the Boy Scouts in the Elks Lodge parking lot like we usually did.

In the photo, Mom, Dad, and I are all squished together by the tree, and a couple steps away from us is Eli: arms tucked all the way into the short sleeves of his Boba Fett shirt, nine, thinning out from the baby fat years, stringy hair, lips blue, mouth upside down. He had made a deal with Mom and Dad that I could pick the tree, and he'd cut it. He wanted to use the saw. He'd always had a thing for sharp stuff.

I picked a good tree—tall and full—and Eli made Mom comb through it to make sure there were no spotted owl nests inside.

"Cut it straight across, straight across," Dad had said.

Eli was belly-down in the snow. "It's hard," he said, slapping at the bottom twigs. "There's all this crap in the way."

"You don't need to use that word," Dad told him. "It's low class, uneducated."

"Okay now," Mom said.

And Dad said, "Just cut the thing."

Three minutes later, he added, "What's going on there? I thought you wanted to do this? I thought it would be easy."

And Eli, his teeth clenched, grunted, "The saw's stuck in the stem."

"We can get a different tree," I suggested. "A smaller one."

"It's a trunk, not a stem," Dad said to Eli. "For Christ's sake, just come out. I'll cut it myself."

"John," Mom told Dad, "let him figure it out. He's doing okay."

"You're always making excuses for him," Dad told her. "There's nothing to figure out. The kid got the saw stuck in the trunk."

Dad pulled Eli from under the tree by the boots. Eli got up and stood there, shivering, his long track of footprints in the snow, while Dad grunted and sawed until the tree toppled over. On our way out, we paid the guy, and Mom asked him to take a picture of us. We took the tree home, and Mom and I decorated it.

After that year, we went back to buying from the Boy Scouts.

FALL

Prompt: Labels.

Today, before class started, Miss Wilson was out in the hall talking to Tae-sung, and we were supposed to be writing, when Brielle showed me a list.

"It's for the party," she whispered. She has to start the list now, she said, because they're only inviting two hundred people, and their parents will KILL them if they get fined again.

The list wasn't the kind a person writes out for Christmas. It was the opposite—a copy of the entire student body here at OLR, alphabetized, with parents' names, addresses, phone numbers, emails, and an *F*, *R*, or *W*. The title on top was "Full, Reduced, or Waived Tuition."

My chest felt like it was caving in. I couldn't breathe. How did Brielle get this list? What would happen if she showed the wrong people, people who didn't care about other people, people who would hurt?

F R W E.

A B C D F.

We really are just letters here.

I looked for my name first. What if I had *W*, or even *R*?

Puakea Keahi was *R*. That was a surprise. She had all those amazing parties.

Fetua Tanielu was *E*. *E* didn't have a meaning.

And along with *F, R, W, E* was another system, too. Colin Silva (*F*) was highlighted in yellow. So were Brielle and Sophia (*F, F*). And the new boy Henley Hollingsworth (*F*). And Eli and Koa and Tate. But not me. And twenty names had been crossed off all the way through with black marker. Isabelle Winters (*R*) was crossed off with one fierce swipe, like Brielle did it when she was annoyed.

"Really?" I whispered, so Isabelle wouldn't hear. She'd gone to the Bransons' Heaven and Hell party last year. What could possibly undo someone from getting to go again?

"It's all over—" Brielle flashed me her phone showing Isabelle's timeline: pictures of Isabelle and Hailey that were just like the ones Li Lu and I used to post—"See, total lesbos."

I was sick. That was mean. And even if it was true, it didn't matter. Isabelle was nice to everyone. She was so chill. I couldn't get why this meant anything to Brielle.

"She's totally into volleyball," Brielle said. "Like, SUPER into it. OBSESSED."

So, what did Brielle have against volleyball? I should have said something. I wanted to say something. I hated myself for not knowing what to say.

"You can tell by their sports bras," Brielle went on. "They wear them EVERYWHERE, all the time, and those skanky booty shorts."

The whole volleyball team wore sports bras and booty shorts. It didn't mean anything. Did the way you dress matter for getting on the Carnivale list?

Was Isabelle crossed off because of spandex? If so, the whole volleyball team would be out. But it wasn't. Ellie Miller, Oliana Rivera, Halia Smith, and Allie Wong weren't crossed off. In fact, the only crossed-off volleyball player was Isabelle.

It was going to feel horrible, being the only one on the team not invited.

Maybe it was a mistake. Maybe Brielle would change her mind.

"Isabelle is completely out?" I whispered to Brielle.

"Yeah, for sure." Brielle didn't pause. "Later, I'll tell you about it, the game."

WINTER

Prompt: Think first: What is your favorite movie right now? Then look back at September 27. Has your favorite movie changed, or is it still the same?

Movies.

Writing about them seems so . . . unimportant. And I've always hated look-backs. I've always thought they were pointless. What are we even doing here, at OLR on O'ahu? What's the reason for writing and memorizing and solving for *x*? What's the purpose of our existence?

What does it matter when you can't even watch your favorite movie the same way anymore? Since December, I've tried watching *The September Issue* a hundred times, and all I see are swirling colors and people talking but not making any sense.

I used to have Anna Wintour's quote all over the place—"Fashion is not about looking back. It's about looking forward." Even after everything, I still think Anna Wintour has that right. The thing I wish she talked more about was HOW to look forward, exactly.

I see *The September Issue* differently now. It still proves that Anna Wintour's a fashion genius, but she's also skeevy and mean to the real artist, Grace Coddington. I don't know how I watched this film so many times before without noticing it was really about Grace, and how amazing her art is, and how hard she works, and how she has to deliver Anna's perfect vision when Anna doesn't even know what she wants.

In the entire documentary, Anna only smiles about four times. She goes around all day worrying about how important scarves and shoes and boots and belts are, which is all wrong. She doesn't even drive herself anywhere—other people chauffer her. Anna has it easy. She doesn't have anything to worry about. She doesn't worry about how she'll survive.

And the designers are obsessed with her. They don't have anything to worry about, either, just fabric and feathers and sequins.

There's all this drama. Over *clothes*.

I used to think it was so real—fashion, friends, Latin, math. Now, I know that none of it is.

None of it can bring back Mom or Li Lu or Koa and Tate.

Everybody is going away.

FALL

Prompt: What is your favorite movie?

What is my favorite movie of all time, ever?

People would think it's *Legally Blonde*. It's kind of old but really funny, and Elle Woods has some amazing looks: low-rise pants with a midriff blouse and beanie, or faux fur and bikini top. Brielle LOVES *Legally Blonde*—she says she's big on the justice system—and I love it, too, it's just not my FAVORITE. And what game is Brielle talking about anyway? And when is she going to tell me?

There's *Leap Year*, which is really romantic (and set in Ireland), about Irish tradition and all that, but it's not my favorite, either.

Girl-war movies are always good, like *Bride Wars*, *Sorority Wars*, and *This Means War*.

But here it is—my favorite movie of all time—*The September Issue*. When I found out about it, it had been out on DVD for a few years already. It's actually a documentary about Anna Wintour, while she puts together the *Vogue* September issue, the single most important piece of print on Planet Earth. Anna talks about how everyone in her family did "important" things, and how she's doing something just as important—art—which she definitely is.

She says, "Fashion is not about looking back. It's always about looking forward."

I mean, that's genius!

Anna always knew she wanted to become the editor of *Vogue*, and she did it. This movie is about more than fashion—it's about making your dreams come true and fighting for what you believe in.

Also, the whole time, you think that Grace Coddington, the creative editor, is not going to come up with anything good enough for the issue. You're on the edge of your seat and biting all your nails, waiting to see if Grace will come through or not. But Anna finally finds some amazing treasures and picks the perfect picture of actor Sienna Miller for the cover, and the issue ends up being absolutely BANANAS.

The Devil Wears Prada is pretty great, too. It's not better than *The September Issue*, though.

The September Issue is pretty much everything.

WINTER

Prompt: Something new in a familiar place.

Last summer, we went to a Bon Festival, Eli and me. Well, we kind of did. Mom was on shift, and Dad had a dinner at the president's house, and I totally said yes when Eli asked me if I wanted to grab a burrito with him. I couldn't remember the last Friday night we had done something together. So unless he was going surfing, which started way too early and took *forever*, I always went with him whenever he asked me to go.

It had been so long, and awkward at first, being somewhere with him on a Friday night. He had hurt his shoulder from a big wave at Sunset a few days before and had to wait a while before getting back out on his board again.

So, Eli and me, we were getting rice-and-bean burritos from Down to Earth on King Street, and he parked on the second story of the garage beside it because there's never any parking on the actual street itself. When we got out of the truck, we heard the festival going on—the bamboo flute, the lute, the koto. It was late July, and a Friday, so of course there was a Bon.

Eli and I had been around Bon Festivals thousands of times, but we had never stopped to really check them out. That night, though, that Friday in July, we got our burritos and ate them inside, and when we were back in the garage after, Eli leaned against the rail and looked down at the little bit of Japan right in the middle of Oʻahu.

We watched that Bon—the dancers raising up their arms as they floated around the red-and-white tent, calling the spirit ghosts to come visit, honoring their ancestors. Lanterns bobbed over them—pinks and greens, yellows and reds—and the flute and lute and koto plinked on.

The sun set out over Diamond Head, and Eli and I watched those dancers float.

A shave ice sounded so good, I thought, *lychee*. My palms were sticky and sweaty on the rail.

But Eli was just watching the dancers, like it was the first time he'd ever seen it, and if I had told him, "Let's go get a shave ice," he would have said, "Nah, let's just head home," because he wanted to party at Tate's, even though Dad told him, "You better not be drinking while you're on those pain pills."

This was it for me, my whole night. I had nothing else to do, nowhere else to go after. Li Lu's mom was making her stay home to study because she was getting a B+ in math, and Eli would never take me to Tate's with him, no way.

The air filled up with Okinawa dango fresh out of the oil, and the smell made me thirstier and dizzy, even. But Eli wasn't going anywhere, and who knew the next Friday night he would take me anyplace. So I stayed right there beside him at the railing, blinking the heat and mascara away from my eyes.

The dancers danced and the lanterns bobbed—pinks and greens, yellows and reds—and the flute and lute and koto plinked on. It was beautiful, the dancers floating around the striped tent. I watched their arms wave slow and soft. I was thinking about Pearl Harbor, ten miles leeward. So much conflict here, so much pain.

Eli, he was watching, too, and I was watching him watch, but he wasn't really seeing, and after a while I noticed he wasn't even thinking. There was literally nothing on his mind. How was that even possible? I didn't realize it then, but I was annoyed by that, jealous even, how he could just *be*. What was that all about?

Eli took in a sharp breath of the heavy dango-scented air: "Swells come in two months," he announced, more to himself than to me.

We were right in the middle of the city, above something so beautiful and complicated, and that's what Eli was "thinking" about. I remember his words, the air, my hands sticky on the rail.

What I've forgotten is my own brother's face.

FALL

Prompt: Describe a memorable field trip.

I really want to know about Brielle's game. Like who's in on it, and can I be in on it, and what do you win at the end. Was Isabelle part of it? But she's not now? Is that why they aren't friends anymore?

Field trips.

We've been to the Bishop Museum, we've hiked Diamond Head, we've gone to the Polynesian Cultural Center, where we stayed the whole day, even for the luau, and didn't get home till eleven. And in sixth grade, my first year here, our class went to Pearl Harbor. It didn't make any sense—how Japan bombed us, then we bombed Japan, then we stuck all the Japanese people who were even born in America into dusty camps, but then we were friends again, after all that. Somehow, Japan moved on and America moved on.

Me, I'm different. People who backstab me, they will never, ever be able to make it right again, not for the rest of forever.

Brother O'Malley, who had just started teaching, let us pick our field trip partners. So of course I picked Li Lu and she picked me. The bus pulled into the enormous lot and parked with all the other buses along the side. We all walked through the lot, toward the flags and past a thousand "reserved" spaces. Back in Oregon, at the library and the grocery stores, there were two or maybe four. But in this lot, there were almost as many saved spaces as regular ones—reserved spots, just for vets. And in the very, very front were other signs—PEARL HARBOR SURVIVOR PARKING ONLY. I remember that. It was happy and sad at the same time.

Our class had tickets for the 10:30 a.m. history movie—I still have mine pinned up on the corkboard behind my bedroom door. So, while we waited for that 10:30 movie, Brother O'Malley tried to keep Kevin Loo away from the water, and Charlie Champion from climbing on the monuments, and Na Wen out of the gift shop. Li Lu and I sat on a bench by the big brass bell, talking about how she liked Oliver Woods and what she should do about it.

The history movie was sad, and I wondered how Laura Yamimoto was doing, sitting there in the theater when there were words like *Jap* in the film. It didn't sound like a good word. Laura cried when we took the boat to the wall with all the names of the soldiers who had died, after Charlie Champion said something to her the rest of us didn't hear. She pulled her long, black hair over her face. She didn't want us to see her crying.

Laura didn't come back to school after that. Some people said her family moved back to Michigan. And Na said she heard Laura transferred to the Koalua Academy of the Arts.

But this island's tiny. You'd think that in two years, Li Lu or I would have seen her somewhere. I hope she got out and started a new life. Even Michigan would be better than here.

FALL

Prompt: Rules.

"It's like *America's Next Top Model*." Brielle slid her Frappuccino over to me, said she didn't want it. ". . . Or *Project Runway*. Or *Top Chef, Chopped*, *American Idol*, *Survivor*, *The Bachelor*, *Amazing Race* . . . You get it, right? You watch those?"

I looked at the Frappuccino, the whip still intact. "Yeah, I watch."

I'd watched all of them. Just last night on *Project Runway*, Elena was eliminated. Michael Kors wasn't thrilled by her looks. I never liked Elena. No one did. But she got eliminated for one literally teeny-tiny thing. BABY clothes. Seriously, you don't even get a chance. One wrong move, and you're out.

"It's a game," Brielle went on, her eyes sparking. "It's fun. Aren't you bored on this fish-kicking island?"

She went on without waiting for me to say, "Totes." "Everyone starts out the same. And then, people get eliminated. They get Cut." Cut with a capital *C*.

I looked over at Isabelle. She was sitting by herself, looking at her phone. Hailey wasn't around. I hadn't seen her since school started up again. Did she even go to OLR anymore?

"Like . . . Isabelle?" I asked.

"Exactly." Brielle leaned into me, and I must have pulled away or something because Brielle put down her phone and said, "Oh god, no, it's not MEAN or anything. It's just a game. People don't even KNOW they're playing it."

"Why did you Cut her?" I asked.

"TAAAYYYLOR," Brielle went on, "I don't Cut anyone, okay? People pretty much Cut themselves. It's like the school decides, or the universe, or whatever. It just happens on its own. It's happening everywhere, all the time."

I had no idea what that meant.

"Okay, fine." She waved her hand in the air. "Isabelle, you know . . . all that drama from Puakea's party . . . She's a dingbat, that's why."

The thing was that Isabelle wasn't a dingbat at all.

Which other people has Brielle Cut? Who were they? What did they do? Why'd they get Cut? What happened to them after? Who besides Brielle and me knew about the game?

"So . . ." Brielle's eyes narrowed like a lizard's. She stood up, put her phone in her bag, and said, "Are you in? Or are you out?"

I wanted to get on Brielle's Carnivale list, to see everyone and talk about it all after, to get my fortune read and see the velvet ottoman, to have an amaretto sour and see the food carts. I thought how great it would be to borrow those Stuart Weitzmans.

And Soo and Noelani, too. Finally, I had more than just one boring friend. I had a group—just like Eli always did. For once, my life was kind of exciting. I had a future. There were so many possibilities.

But those good, happy things were instantly erased by the panic that came next. What would happen if I didn't play? Would I be Cut?

Brielle and I wouldn't be friends anymore? If so, she'd take Soo and Noelani with her. I'd lose everything.

"Think about it," Brielle told me. She picked up the Frappuccino she had given me and clutched it to her chest. Then she walked off to stand out in the courtyard with Noelani and Soo.

WINTER

Prompt: If you could change one thing about yourself, what would it be?

Schools.

Of course I would change that night at Pipeline, too. I'd beg Eli not to go when Stacy texted him. I'd come up with some excuse about why he had to stay.

Actually, I wouldn't have gone to that party in the first place. I would change that, too.

I'd change ever even talking to Brielle that day back in September. About All of My Purple Life. About Eli.

But changing schools, that's what I'd do right now. I'd get out of Our Lady of Redemption, and I would go somewhere—anywhere—else.

Trash.

That was on my locker door, scribbled in lipstick, Fuchsia Flash matte.

Trash. It's a terrible, horrible word.

It means you don't matter at all.

"Taylor?" Sister Anne asked. "Do you know who did this?"

I am dying. Part by part. Cell by cell. I can't do anything to stop it.

And even though I'm dying, the math and history homework keeps coming.

Last night, when Dad was sitting in the green chair watching about Mars on *Nightly News*, I asked him for a list of reasons for the "sharp political divide in America."

Dad told me, "Everyone has their own agenda."

"Is there also another reason?" I asked.

Mr. Montalvo wasn't going to keep giving me full credit for one-answer "lists."

"There are two kinds of people," Dad said to his second sloe and tonic or maybe even his third, "Democrats and Republicans—"

"Can I switch schools?" I just asked him straight out.

"Why?" he asked me. He seemed surprised. And kind of irritated.

Sinking down into the other green chair, I thought about why—ALL the reasons why—I had to switch schools: the Smashbox Fuchsia Flash *Trash* on my locker, Brielle, math, Li Lu. How the whole health class turned around and stared at me at the start of the "Alcohol, Decisions, and You" lesson.

I told Dad, "It's . . . hard."

After a while, Dad asked, "Where?"

"School," I told him. "School is hard. It was hard going back, and it's been one month and twenty-five days, and it's still completely impossible."

"Not where is it hard," he said. "Where would you want to go?"

I hadn't really thought about where I would go. I had just thought about the leaving.

"Malala, maybe?" It was a random suggestion. But anywhere away from Brielle and Soo and Li Lu and Sister Anne and Colin Silva would be better than Our Lady of Redemption. Anywhere away from the two empty desks in the back of English 12, three if you counted the one Eli used to sit in.

While Dad kept his eyes on Scott Pelley, I took a second to try to sound convincing while also not over the top. I didn't want to give Dad a reason to leave.

Dad cupped his chin in his hand, rubbed his thumb back and forth like a windshield wiper. "Our Lady of Redemption is a great school, Taylor. It's worth sticking it out. You can use it as a springboard to get into any college."

"To the mainland? With Grammie?" I knew he'd never go for that.

"That's not happening."

"You can homeschool me? It will be like I'm in college, in one of your classes. I'll do all the work, every assignment, I promise, and I'll practice the Sonatina every day, too."

I could do better. I was eight chapters and summaries behind on *To Kill a Mockingbird*, and I had gotten a D+ on the geometry test and a 61 percent in Latin.

I could google ways to improve memory.

Dad sighed a long, slow sigh. "There are two kinds of people in the world, Taylor," he said again. "People who get through things, and people who give up. And Harpers don't give up. You like your teachers, and you'll be with all your friends."

I thought about Brielle and her Fuchsia Flash matte lips today, blowing me a kiss as she swished by my locker after school. Wingnut, birdbrain, bubblehead . . . Brielle Branson knew the meanest compound words on earth.

That's how Dad and I left things. That we don't give up. That OLR's great. That I'm with all my friends.

FALL

Prompt: Natural selection.

The new Bachelor is Sean Lowe. I read it in *People*, and I can't wait! It's premiering in three months and six days, and Chris Harrison said it is going to be "the most dramatic season ever."

During the summer, Emily gave Jef and Arie roses, and sent Sean off *The Bachelorette*. Probably, she eliminated him because he turned down her overnight date card. He's just not that guy. Hopefully this season, he finds somebody amazing. In the end, people always get what they deserve.

Sister Anne pulled me into her office. Again. This time, she asked if I knew anything about the tuition list that had gotten out.

I could see it on her computer, the Instagram page called "OLR X-posed."

Sister Anne knew I didn't know anything—I don't know anything anymore. She didn't ask me any more questions about it. She told me to have a drink of water before I went back to math.

When I got home, I pulled up the page and read all the posts about who was on full or reduced or waived tuition. No one could figure out Fetua's *E*. There were a lot of guesses, like *Exception*, or *Exchange*.

People were obsessed with Puakea. They were horrible, mean. They wrote things like "leech" under a picture of her with sunglasses on, and “mooch” under a picture of her on a surfboard, and “freeloader” under a picture of her with a piña colada at the Waikiki Yacht Club.

And then there was the picture of her with her mom and dad, the three of them at a wedding at the Ko Olina Marina.

Underneath was the word Bubblehead.

WINTER

Prompt: Does reality TV reflect authentic American culture?

Today, there are two white birds in the hibiscus. Tern found another tern. Even the tern has someone.

The February rain knocked a lot of the flowers on to the ground. There are more flowers on the pavement than in the branches.

I'm in class. Writing words. Using class time wisely.

Reality shows.

They're not the whole story, not the whole truth. People don't know what led up to that one thing, or the reason someone did what they did. They don't remember the person was good inside. They forget all about who the person was, and they remember just the one thing they did, the one thing that makes them who they are from then on, who they'll always be.

Our house doesn't smell the same as it used to.

Every day after school, I notice it more and more—the oldness, the hot. It smells . . . dead. And smother-y. I open up all the blinds and windows, and I let in the trade winds, the ocean salt and rain and plumeria, and then the house smells kind of like before.

But I forgot to open the house yesterday, and the bad smell was everywhere.

And after that tuition list scandal at OLR, I've been thinking about tuition. Money. Our house. How did we ever buy this house way up in Mānoa? How do we pay for the view of Honolulu, the quiet street, two stories, the big garden?

Miss Wilson doesn't have a house like this, I'm sure. And she's a teacher, like Dad. And Mom couldn't possibly make enough as a hospice nurse to afford this. She didn't even work those years she was on the waiting list to get on another waiting list to go to nursing school here.

There is literally only one way this is possible. It's the same way Eli and I pay full tuition at school. Someone has been making our lives happen for us.

It didn't feel good to know that. It didn't feel . . . right.

Neither did the Brielle stuff. She was getting really mean. Dangerous. It was one thing calling people names behind their backs, or writing words that didn't even make sense on their locker. But this was a whole other level—plastering their money business everywhere.

After Dad sabotaged my idea to change schools, I flipped through the February issue of *Elle* that had come a couple weeks ago, the one with the Annual Reader's Choice Beauty Awards. And there was this one ad for a watch—a guy in some board shorts, with long, salty bangs and sand on his shoulders but with the wrong eyes and jaw, and not as skinny. He was smiling on a beach. I couldn't tell where the beach was, exactly, because it's mostly just water, and water looks pretty much the same everywhere. But I could see that he was happy.

Really carefully, I cut that guy away from the water and off the page, and I put him on the wall up over my bed. Tape wouldn't stick to the wall, and no one can ever find a tack around here, so I had to staple Almost-Eli once in the foot, and once in the arm, and once at the top of his head.

FALL

Prompt: Revenge.

It turns out, the attacks weren't because of a movie. It was actually revenge. That's what CNN said.

The worst thing about revenge is when people think it's done in the name of justice, of making things even and right.

Playing or not playing Brielle's pointless game isn't really a choice.

I have to play it. Because if I don't, I could end up like Puakea on some hate page dedicated to making my life completely miserable, plus Li Lu totally started a fight with me last night, and Brielle and Soo and Noelani are all I have now.

Out of nowhere, Li Lu texted: *Brielle is totally using u*

And: *u kno it's true u just dont wanna admit it*

And: *u dont even know what a real friend is anymore*

that's totally false, I texted back: *u have no idea what ur talking abt*

And: *why do u even care?*

Her: *i know u better than anyone*

And: *she totally has an agenda*

And: *i don't kno what it is or why shes using u but she is*

And: *she bought u. with lip gloss. u sold out.*

Now, Li Lu was definitely making this an issue.

Me: *u looooovvvve drama! ur always in everybodys face!*

Her: *u think ur so much better than everybody else now*
And: *u know shes using u. u just dont want to believe it*
And: *u don't even know who u are anymore*
Me: *u don't want me to have any other friends*
And: *its always been like that*
And: *u always try to control everything*
Her: *whats so great abt Brielle anyway?*
Me: *for one thing she doesn't tell me how to live my life*
And: *for another thing, people actually LIKE her*
My phone was quiet for a long time.
Then her: *fine. whatever. be friends w/ her or me but not both of us*
Me: *FINE. if thats how it is. if ur forcing me to choose i pick her*

There was nothing else after that. From either of us.

I took the "Forever" heart locket from around my neck and told myself to get rid of it.

WINTER

Prompt: Oops.

Last night, out of nowhere, Henley texted me two words: *Chicken piccata*.

There was a picture of the cat after that, its little pink tongue sticking out toward a mound of meat, cream sauce, and those green caper things.

I was shocked. I mean, we hadn't been talking at all. Then this.

so? u and Jasmine? I texted back, instantly wishing I hadn't.

And him: *um . . . definitely not.*

I knew he wasn't lying. Brielle had lied that day at lunch.

I changed the subject, wanting to keep things going: *What are u into?*

Oh god. I read it back to myself. *What are u into?* No, no, no . . . *Into*. That's not what I meant. I meant to ask what he was UP to! *Into* made it seem like I was asking if he was into girls or guys or what.

So. Silly.

I waited to hear back. I waited a long time. And the longer I waited, the sillier it sounded.

Of ALL the things I could have asked him, I had asked him the silliest thing in the world.

I can't talk to him now. I just have to push it all out of my mind.

On every level, every day here gets worse and worse and worse.

Yesterday after school, I saw Macario with his surfboard. His shoes were already off.

Since Koa and Tate and Eli are all gone, Macario's been coming to school a lot more. I guess he has no one to skip with anymore.

"Hey, Grommet," he told me, "I'll catch a big one for your bruddah."

This time of year, the swells are huge. For a second, I thought Eli would be sad he's missing it.

Then I remembered to hate myself for feeling sorry for him. I remembered what he did.

FALL

Prompt: Decisions.

Today, Brielle came up to my locker and sprayed me with White Gardenia Petals. "Taylor Harper," she said, "you might make a girl think you've been avoiding her or something."

I don't know why Brielle would say that. She herself had been missing a ton of school. I saw Soo's post to her Instagram: "Boo, when u coming back?"

For three whole days, I didn't see a single swish of Brielle's macadamia hair or get one whiff of her perfume.

I tried to throw back my head and laugh her off, like I'd seen her do a thousand times.

"That's quite a system." Brielle pointed to my locker. "Everything in perfect order . . . So, anyway, are you in?"

Li Lu had completely bailed on me. I messed things up again with Henley. Brielle and Noelani and Soo were the only friends I had left in the world. It was just better to play Brielle's meaningless game. It wasn't going to go anywhere, and anyway, no one was going to find out about it.

"How does it work?" I shut my locker door.

Brielle was smiling. "For a second there," she said, "I thought you were going to tell me you were out." She did the lizard eyes thing.

"There aren't a ton of rules," she said. "Basically, we wait. We watch. Does she Cut herself, or does she make it onto the Carnivale list?"

The way Brielle said it, I already knew. She had someone picked out. For me to watch.

"Who is it?" I asked.

Our eyes locked.

Brielle said, "Noelani."

WINTER

Prompt: Can something be wrong and also right?

Yesterday, after school, I walked up North King to Bank of Hawaii and took some money out of my college savings. The teller told me I had to have a parent signature, but Dad would never let me touch that money—not even for something this important—and Mom was still in bed. So I told the teller I'd run the slip out to the car and have my mom sign, and I'd be right back. This is where living in Hawaii is a plus. People aren't all wound up about things.

Only, I went around to the side and signed "Julia Harper" almost exactly like Mom would do herself. When it was all done, I had $200 in my purse, enough for the teriyaki dinner I'm going to make for Mom and Dad, plus enough for laundry soap and a few weeks of lunches. I thought I'd pass on the birds of paradise. Just in case I needed that money in the future.

On my way home, I got a text from Henley: *cooking.*

So it wasn't all over???

This time before writing back, I actually thought for a second. Then I texted: *i like 2 cook 2, Im making my family dinner 2morrow!*

The exclamation mark was a little much. I swapped it out with a regular period and added: *What do u make?*

Him: Happy face/tongue stuck out.

Then: *Coconut soup.*

Me: *Seriously???*

Henley's *yaai* (who wasn't really his technical grandma, but his stepmom's mom) lived in Thailand, Henley texted. She came to visit and taught him how to make it. She even planted a tree in their yard to make fresh kefir.

I had no idea what a kefir was.

Me: *are u Team Kristen or Brooke*

He came back with a ???

Me: *Top Chef?!? Finale tomorrow*

Maybe we could watch it together.

It was getting dark. The sun was gone, the moon rising up over Mānoa.

I waited a long time, but Henley never got back to me. Had I said the wrong thing again? I read through the whole thread twice. It didn't seem like it. But you could never know for sure.

FALL

Prompt: Listen to this song and write what or how it makes you think or feel. (Gavin DeGraw, "Soldier")

Miss Wilson said that every so often, she'll play songs for us to write about.

Today, she is: black wide-leg pants, pink top in woodblock print. MAKE IT MAJOR: Add a cropped jacket and colorful flats. Streamline the look with straightened hair and long earrings.

This is a decent song. It's not the kind of music I usually listen to, and I don't see how it's about soldiers. Is it supposed to make us think about the Middle East?

Civil war.

People fighting each other.

The whole point of Brielle's game is to get dirt on her best friend?

That day before fourth period at my locker, when she sprayed me with White Gardenia Petals, she said a girl could never be sure about anyone.

Noelani, though?

Everyone loves Noelani. She's popular, happy, friendly. Nice. She has great style, money, and is student-body secretary. Even teachers love her.

I can't imagine Noelani would do ANYTHING to be the Next Cut. But also, I had wondered that about Isabelle. No one was safe.

Like always, Brielle could tell I wasn't one hundred percent.

"I thought you two were close," I said.

"The people closest to us are EXACTLY the ones we shouldn't be one hundred percent sure about," Brielle whispered while Miss Wilson started up the song. "It's about trust. I have to know EVERYTHING, so I can be prepared."

Prepared for what, I wondered.

"Stalk her," Brielle went on. "I mean . . . don't STALK her, stalk her. But . . . you know . . . friend her, follow her, see what she's really about."

And honestly, this whole thing makes me nervous.

Yesterday, after school, I had a friend request on Facebook and another on Instagram.

Both of them were from Soo.

WINTER

Prompt: Revisit the argument you made in October. Do you still feel the same way?

I have to get my math grade up. The tutor just gives me the answer to the problems. He doesn't really explain how to do them, and Dad is going to lose it.

Last night, after I finished studying for the Latin quiz, I made the teriyaki chicken.

I went into Mom's room and told her dinner would be ready in twenty minutes. I turned on her shower, told her the water was ready. But after the rice was boiling, the water was still running, and Mom was still in bed. Her phone was on her nightstand, plugged in, ringing.

"Do you want me to answer it?" I asked her.

It was some number with a 406 area code. Where was that? Was it something about Eli?

Mom didn't answer. She didn't even move, but the shower water kept running and running. Finally, the phone stopped ringing.

I sat down on the bed.

"I made us dinner," I said. "Teriyaki and rice."

She said she'd eat later. Her phone beeped twice with a new voicemail.

"Would you like me to play it?" I asked.

There were seventeen voicemails. Were any of them about Eli? Were any of them *not* about Eli?

"No thank you," Mom said. She was going to sleep for a little while.

I pulled up her quilt, turned off the shower.

"Tay?" Mom mumbled. "You can have my seahorses."

She was talking about the earrings she'd bought herself at the farmer's market when we first came. She never bought anything for herself, and she loved those so much. They were not seahorse shaped but sterling discs that dropped down and were stamped with seahorses. I ALWAYS wanted those earrings, not because I liked them—they weren't my style—but because Mom did. She thought they were pretty and special. So I'd always thought they must be, too.

But now I was sick about them. I didn't want those seahorses, and I wasn't going to take them. I was going to leave them in that little cedar box right there.

"Have a good sleep, Mom," I whispered, closing the door.

The dinner was starting out all wrong. Because I didn't know how to work the barbecue, I had to bake the chicken, and it came out dry and rubbery. Also, the rice was undercooked—gummy and chewy.

Dad didn't come home from playing handball till late, and when he did, he said he'd already grabbed a sandwich at the college. He took off his tie, sat in the green armchair, pulled his ringing phone out of his shirt pocket, and looked at it as it rang. It stopped, then it started ringing again, and Dad made a face and hit the ANSWER button hard with his thumb.

"Hello, Stella," Dad said, like he was giving a concession speech, throwing in the towel.

I pretended I was cleaning up the dinner, scrubbed the sauce that was burned into the bottom of the pan, but the hot water had run out because of the marathon shower Mom never took.

"We're all fine." Dad was drawing out his words. "Busy here, just busy."

Later, I tried to do my math. But I kept thinking about the seahorses. And I wondered why Dad had lied like that to Grammie Stella. So I switched to Latin, but I couldn't remember any of the Latin I was supposed to remember. Instead, I put two pieces of bread in the toaster and started the lilikoi tea.

A lot has changed since October, but homework has stayed the same. I still think kids shouldn't have to do it. Living is hard enough.

FALL

Prompt: Does homework help or hurt kids?

After school, kids' brains are fried. We just want to eat and hang out at home or with friends. Mostly, homework is memorizing stuff we forget right after the test, or it's reading that doesn't sink in because there's already too much crammed in our minds. Kids have way more to think about than extra schoolwork.

I know that other countries think homework is important, like China and Japan. But France doesn't. And I'm with France.

Look at famous people like Lady Gaga, for example. Did she get where she is by doing homework?

If Steve Jobs had been doing a bunch of math instead of putting together computer parts in his garage, there would be no Apple. If Kurt Cobain had been reading *To Kill a Mockingbird* instead of playing with his garage band, the whole grunge movement would never have happened.

Fetua does all her homework. And where is it getting her? If she wasn't doing math and Latin, maybe she'd be the next big author, the next John Green.

"I can't believe this."

That's the first line from my favorite book, *Queen of Babble*.

This book gives fashion the props it deserves. I mean, the whole story *begins* with fashion! The main character, Lizzie (the Lizzie

Broadcasting System, because she talks so much), spends a summer in London with her loser boyfriend. But she ends up going to France to work at a château and has all this boy drama with Luke and all this friend drama, too.

It seems pretty real. Lizzie is a huge risk-taker—something I definitely admire about people. She's also brave and HILARIOUS! At first, she has absolutely no idea what she's going to do after she graduates! She'll figure it out, though. There are two more books in the series—thank you, mullet baby Jesus.

Me, I know what I want to do. When I graduate from design school in Portland, I'm going to France and New York, just like Lizzie.

I read this book in two days, then lent it to Li Lu, who said Lizzie was annoying. (Li Lu prefers reading about vampires.) She never finished it—or gave it back to me, now that I think about it.

Also, I can't find the cord that connects my iPod to the computer—the short white one.

Seriously, I can't find it anywhere. So (1) I can't charge it, and (2) I can't make a new playlist. I would borrow Eli's cord, but his room is such a mess I'd never be able to find it. And also, Eli would kill me if he knew I was in there.

Dad said my cord is probably right where I left it. Mom told me it would show up somewhere.

I looked all over my room.

After, of course, I checked the freezer.

Seriously. I'm going to kill Eli.

FALL

Prompt: Should the drinking age in Hawaii stay at twenty-one, or should it be changed back to eighteen?

The drinking age doesn't matter. Anyway, it's getting to be more and more about weed.

People come to Hawaii to party. When you think "Hawaii," you think beaches and mai tais, bars, hotels, restaurants, the college, the base—there's nothing else to do, really. We're all trapped. We might as well have a good time while we're stuck here.

Koa has a ginormous supply of Malibu and Cuervo right at his house. And at Puakea Keahi's last weekend, there were two kegs and Jäger. Everyone was talking about it. People posted pictures all over.

Speaking of parties, Sophia booked the band! For Carnivale. It's Hula-baloo, who EVERYONE loves. Island music. So. Good! Carnivale is literally only eighty days away.

The Five-0 should let people make their own decisions. They should worry about bigger problems, like the ice that's all over here. That's the real problem.

Seriously. We're just trying to live our lives.

And speaking of drinking, I asked Brielle if she wanted to get a Frappuccino after school.

She slammed her locker door, left a full can of Red Bull Sugarfree spinning on the floor, and said Frappuccinos were for bubbleheads.

That was harsh. I asked what her deal was, and she said her dad was a jackhole. She asked to go with him on his business trip to Australia. She needed a break, she'd told him. But for no reason, her dad said no.

Brielle hates that word.

She said it was total crap, that there was no reason her dad couldn't bring her. He couldn't even come up with ONE.

Honestly, she was making such a big deal out of it all. So she can't go to Australia right now. Geez, you'd think her whole life was ruined.

Last night on *Project Runway*, Sonjia was eliminated because of the dress she made. Okay, it looked a little like lettuce. But did the judges have to be so mean about it? First Tim Gunn made Sonjia feel like a loser. Then Michael Kors called her work "an ice skating costume." That was unnecessary, over-the-top brutal.

WINTER

Prompt: "How do I love thee? Let me count the ways . . ."
(Elizabeth Barrett Browning, 1806–1861)

Miss Wilson asked if I would consider stopping by Ticket to Write. Just to check it out.

The Writing Club? Fetua's group?

"Oh, I don't know," I told her.

"Your writing is really improving," Miss Wilson said. "Your *Mockingbird* essays are descriptive, detailed." She told me I'm showing the bigger picture, a deeper understanding. It's been happening in history, too. Mr. Montalvo said that my essays are clearer now, more organized. None of this makes any sense. My life definitely doesn't feel clear or organized. And I don't understand anything.

Miss Wilson told me Ticket to Write is once a month, that I could think about it. Dad would probably love it if I joined. That would be some points with him, at least.

Yesterday, the Bank of Hawaii on King Street called him at the college to verify that Mom had signed the bank withdrawal slip I'd forged to get that chicken at Foodland. The truth is that I'm running out of money.

Bankoh had been having some problems lately, they said. They were just being careful.

Dad covered for me, or maybe for himself. He said that yes, his wife had signed, she must've been in a hurry.

I thought I was going to get grounded for a month, or, in the best case, a big lecture.

But I got this instead: "Taylor, I'd expect this from Eli, but I wouldn't expect it from you."

I let that go, asked Dad instead if he was taking Mom to Alan Wong's like he always did on Valentine's Day.

He looked surprised. Had he forgotten what day it was?

He told me it was too late to make a reservation.

"She'd like noodles." I tried to help Dad with a backup plan. My own Valentine's Day might be nonexistent—it's been forever since Henley's texted—but I could save Mom and Dad's. "Italian? Indian? Mexican? Thai?"

I was hoping the more ideas I'd had, the better chance Dad had of taking Mom out.

"Taylor, it's too late," he told me.

FALL

Prompt: What's something about O'ahu most folks don't know?

Mongooses.

Most people have no idea about those here.

A long time ago, O'ahu brought in mongooses from Jamaica to catch the rats that were eating all the sugarcane. But the mongooses didn't eat the rats because they weren't nocturnal. Instead, they ate birds and eggs. So now, there are almost no Nenes.

"I have to know," Brielle told me at lunch. She told Noelani and Soo she needed to talk to me alone. "About Noelani. Is there anything on her?"

"Not really," I said.

Brielle's shoulders slumped. She sighed. "Are you looking EVERYWHERE? At EVERYTHING, at ALL her Facebook and Instagram posts?"

"I friended her," I said. I mean, I was doing what I could do. And anyway, Brielle was best friends with her. She had way more access to that stuff than I did. Brielle should know better than anyone that there's nothing on Noelani.

This game is the worst. I wish I could get out of it. You have to do every single thing perfectly. There's no room—not even one millimeter—for a single, small fail. You have to watch everything all the time. You have to watch yourself.

Instead of posting selfies with Li Lu that Soo would tell Brielle about—selfies that would definitely get me Cut for liking girls or something—I've been putting up pictures that are safe. The underneath of a banana tree leaf, a cat curled up by a FERAL CATS sign, Eli waxing a board at Dave's Waves.

It seemed like Noelani was doing the same thing—there weren't any pictures of her, just of memes. No one could possibly make anything bad out of a picture of Duke's hula pie. Hula pie is everything: a chunk of chocolate cookie crust around macadamia ice cream, topped off with dripping chocolate, nuts, and whipped cream.

I shook my head. "Really," I said to Brielle. "There's really nothing."

Brielle came back fast. "Get it together, Taylor," she said. "No one is perfect. Try harder."

"Hey," Brielle added as she walked away, "have you accepted Soo's friend request?"

"What?" I said. "Not yet. I forgot."

"What are you waiting for?" Brielle called back over her shoulder. "You know, you should really get on that."

WINTER

Prompt: What is the real O'ahu?

Eli got the best parts of Mom—the eyelashes, the legs. I got the worst of her, the parts no one can see. Those are the inside parts, the sad ones.

There's another side to O'ahu—Mom has shown Eli and me. There's leeward, windward, mauka, makai . . . And then there's the sad side—Pua Lane and Wahiawa Heights.

Even in Honolulu's heart, high-rises tower over banyans and beaches, their air conditioners thinning out the ozone. Horns honk and mufflers fire down University. Buses screech to a stop and peel away again, and jackhammers bite tirelessly at the pavement.

People move here expecting paradise—palm trees and pulled pork, sunsets and slack-key. Some people come, some people go. And some folks are stuck here. They can't make their lives happen. Bread that gets moldy right when the bag opens is $7 for Brielle and for Fetua.

The real O'ahu's not about mai tais at the Royal Hawaiian.

Yes, there is that, and the flowers and the swells like Pipeline that make you cry.

Sure the shopping's amazing, and the coconut pie. Flip-flops are standard footwear, and everyone still stacks the bangles Queen Lili'uokalani trended a hundred years ago. The traditions go forward and back.

But also, Oʻahu is fire engines, ice heads. It's the no-teeth people pushing carts in Mōʻiliʻili, their scuffed-up shoes parked under tarps. It's old kamaʻāina with shriveled arms and hunched backs—crossing the street, serving up loco mocos, bagging groceries at Foodland.

A week ago, I asked Dad about it. He was pouring coffee during a commercial on the KHON2 morning news. Me, I was thinking about the security guard at school, the one we got the day before winter break.

I asked Dad, "Why are there so many hurt people here?"

And when Dad asked what I meant, I said, "So many people here, on Oʻahu, they're shriveled and they're hunched."

I had never noticed before. So many people, shriveled and sad. How had I never noticed that?

Dad put down the coffeepot. He looked at the top of my head, like he was thinking maybe I had gotten taller or something.

"It's been that way a long time," he said. "Maybe fetal alcohol syndrome, or lack of prenatal care, or fallout from the Bikini Atoll bomb testing in the '40s, or . . ."

Even Dad didn't have an answer.

Complicated, that's the real Oʻahu.

It's splatters of betel nut spit at the bus stops along Kalākaua. For the longest time, I thought Oʻahu was bleeding. Now I know it is, for sure.

The real Oʻahu is domestic-abuse hotlines on bulletin boards in the post office, and $13 boxes of corn flakes, and shells of abandoned cars, their parts all stripped by thieves. It's overripe mangoes falling on the roofs of tutus' homes. It's traffic and car alarms, cheap beer and souvenirs made in China.

It's bikes that rust because of salt and rain.

The real O‘ahu is beyond waterfalls and rainbows—reds and yellows and pinks and greens, its blue sea and buttery sun fading every day from being ruled over but forgotten—maybe ignored—by the mainland.

The real O‘ahu cries at once for rescue and independence.

It’s the geckos, clinging to the windows at night, trying to hold on.

FALL

Prompt: "Nice guys finish last."
(Leo Durocher, Manager of the Brooklyn Dodgers, 1946)

It was Fashion Week on *Project Runway*! Jennifer Hudson was the judge, and Dmitry won, even though everyone thought Fabio would.

Chris panicked because he knew he was going to lose. And he just couldn't cope. He started unraveling and couldn't stop. He got in this huge fight with Melissa about what color her fabric was, then made fun of her.

Dmitry, though, he got along with everyone. For him, it was about survival. He was basically homeless. His English wasn't great. He HAD to win. And he did. His architecture collection was genius! Completely visionary—using the Lord & Taylors to accessorize.

Do nice guys finish last?

No.

Obviously, nice guys finish first.

The whole season, Chris was a complete jackhole, and he totally lost.

Eventually, bad people get what's been coming to them.

What is Isabelle swirling on and on about? She definitely has a lot to say about this prompt.

* * *

"Have you found anything?" Brielle asked me. Again. She DOES NOT give up.

I thought about Noelani, her thick, dark hair—wavy and long. How she pinned it all back with the violet orchid when she was Homecoming royalty. What would Brielle do if she knew?

My own scalp was itchy everywhere, and I made my hands into fists to keep from scratching.

"Everyone has something," Brielle said. "Everyone."

"Haven't you two been friends forever, though?" I said. "Wouldn't you pretty much know everything about each other? Don't you tell each other everything?"

Brielle bit her Colorbar Peach Crush lip. She looked at the floor.

Behind my ear got prickly, and my eyebrows, too. I could scratch for just a second, and she'd never know. But, if she did see, she'd think I had it, too.

Brielle's eyes flashed. "The things we DON'T know, Taylor, the things people don't say, what they hide, that is the most dangerous."

She could tell I knew something. Even though it wasn't really anything. It should have meant nothing to Brielle. But it was everything to Noelani. She'd be wrecked by it for sure.

"And people who know things about other people," Brielle went on, "the ones who keep important information to themselves, well, those people are just pure spineless."

Not telling Brielle about Noelani was terrifying. If she found out I knew and didn't tell her, which she would, she'd hate me, Cut me, make my life miserable.

"It's nothing, really." I rubbed my palms into my eyes, hoping she would just drop the whole thing.

“Taylor.” Brielle pulled my hands from my face. “What. Do. You. Know?”

I was in it now. Brielle Branson had brought me into the game—I had let her—and she was counting on me. What happened when you backstabbed the richest, most popular girl in eighth grade? You basically died. That’s what.

Noelani. I could not get out of my mind what she looked like when the Safeway checker asked if she wanted a bag the other night. Mom and I were at Safeway getting vanilla to make banana bread, and Noelani was in front of us.

At first, she looked away fast, pretending she didn’t see us, pretending we weren’t there. But then the checker asked Mom how her garden was, and Noelani had to turn and look. She said hi, but her eyes were all shifty, and she turned away.

I thought that was random. Noelani was always happy to talk to everyone.

But it made sense when the checker slid the box across the scanner.

I could either not tell or tell Brielle.

Noelani had lice.

WINTER

Prompt: Do professional athletes deserve the salaries they make?

On Saturday, when I got up, it smelled like pancakes!

Mom was in the kitchen, making banana pancakes, and the coconut syrup was right there on the counter! And Dad was sitting in his green chair, watching the KHON2 morning news and drinking his coffee. It seemed he had moved past the bank thing. Everything was back the way it was before.

Mom was wearing a tank top and shorts, and her knees were stained with dirt.

"Look at the lilliko'i!" She took me out and showed me a new passion fruit vine. A flower was already bursting vibrantly in purple and yellow. Mom said she was drying some leaves in the kitchen. In a few days, she'd be able to make tea.

I asked her what had happened to the old vine, and she waved toward a pile of stems by the steps. They were all withered and black.

"Snails," she said. She asked what I was going to do today.

When I told her I didn't have any plans, she asked if I wanted to go to the farmer's market.

"The Kapi'olani one?" I asked. That was the one on Saturdays, the best one, the biggest, the one with the Kona Latte Ono Pops!

We went. Mom let me pick out the birds of paradise to put in the elephant vase, just like before, and we got eight—my lucky number—even though Mom taught me forever ago that you should always arrange flowers in odd numbers.

It really was the best day ever.

That's why I'm writing this down. In my notebook. Because yesterday was such a good day, and I want to remember it forever—the day Mom got better.

WINTER

Prompt: What is your dream job?

I thought Mom was better. She WAS better. She made pancakes.

But now, she's not better. She's tired again. Maybe it's from the weekend, from all that shopping at the farmer's market? I should have noticed. I should have told her, *Let's go back home*. She waited for me forever while I stood in the Ono Pop line.

Dad said this thing with Mom has to stop. He told her that. He shook out a couple different-colored pills from some bottles on her nightstand, and held out a glass of water, and said, "Take these."

He said that in a voice I've never heard from him before, not even with Eli.

It has to stop—or what? What was Dad going to do if Mom didn't take those pills? If she didn't get better?

Mom doesn't like pills. She drinks tea, and rubs aloe on sunburns and arnica on bruises, and gives me little pieces of ginger candy when my stomach hurts.

It doesn't make sense. Mom made pancakes. She bought birds of paradise that are still in the elephant vase on the table. She was better.

"Can you close the blinds all the way?" Mom pulled the quilt right up to her chin.

While Dad was standing there, by Mom, by the pills, Mom's phone was ringing and ringing again. Over the ringing, Dad was saying, "You can do this, Julia. You have to make up your mind to do it. You got through this once. You can do it again."

Eighteen years ago, when Eli was born in Oregon right before winter hit, Mom got the blues. Grammie Stella told me about it.

One day in sixth grade, I was sad, and Grammie Stella was visiting, and I told her I was sad. I didn't know why I was sad. I had a mom, a dad, a brother, and a house. It wasn't about having, or wanting. It was about BEING. I was just being sad.

Grammie Stella was staying at the Hilton Village, and she bought me a bubble tea—a coconut taro one.

"I'm kind of . . . sad," I told her when she asked how I was doing. I was sad, and I didn't know why.

"Well, keep your eye on things," Grammie told me. "Your grandpa Olie, he got the blues, and once he got them, he never quite shook them." She said Mom got the blues after Eli was born, and they knocked her out for quite some time.

I can't remember Grandpa Olie, but Eli does. He always told me how Grandpa would come out on the front steps when we knocked, saying, "It's my little huckle-buckles!" He always had a glass bowl of baby Butterfingers on the table.

"How'd she get rid of them?" I had asked Grammie.

"You know your mom," Grammie said. "She wouldn't take anything, so . . . time. It just took time, is all."

The trouble with time is that it's immeasurable.

Under her breath, Grammie added, "And your dad just went right on with his work."

Since that talk with her in the Hilton Village, I've panicked when Mom has looked worried or sad. I don't want the blues to steal her away again.

This thing with Eli isn't the first time I've worried. But it's definitely the most.

And I'm scared for me, too. I don't want to be like Mom, like Eli. And I think I might be. How is that going to end up for everyone?

FALL

Prompt: Family.

"Let's all say 'Up your butt' whenever someone asks something!" Eli was smiling wide.

Mom called from the kitchen, "Who knows where my big spatula went?"

And Eli said, "Up your butt!"

Mom laughed. "Right, I forgot to look there," and Eli and I laughed, too.

Then Dad peeked over the *Honolulu Star-Advertiser* and told us, "That's enough of that now."

Last year for his friends for Christmas, Eli made a slideshow—Top Ten Christmas Hotties. Mrs. Claus came in at number ten, Betty Boop at four, the Victoria's Secret Angels at two, and Mary the Virgin Mother of Christ at the top.

He sticks everything in the freezer—our toothbrushes, my bathing suit top, the Scotch tape. When Mom "lost" her big spatula, that's right where it was.

When they aren't surfing, Eli and Koa and Tate and Macario go back and forth and back and forth and back and forth between Koa's house and ours (if Dad has a night class or a meeting) playing Rock Band, with Eli on drums, Koa and Macario on vocals, and Tate on guitar. They pick different female avatars, but they play the same song every time—Metallica's "Enter Sandman." And after they fail (a.k.a. EVERY time), they sweep all the food out of the fridge and the cupboards into a brown bag, and they cram into Koa's Jeep for Bowls or Sandys or—if there's even kind of enough light—they head up to the North.

"Come with us, Grom!" Eli calls to me over his shoulder, board under his arm, pockets stuffed with wax.

"I have homework," I say.

"Who gives a rat's *** about homework?" Eli calls back.

He always leaves the door open.

WINTER

Prompt: There are more ways than ever to communicate . . .

It's not good.

Mom is still in bed. Her room is dark. Rotten and stale, like Mom never got up and made pancakes.

"Are you just waiting on the trade winds?" I asked Mom.

I opened up her blinds, and I lay down to wait, too.

While Mom slept, a hibiscus-y breeze blew through the screen, and the chimes outside clanked into each other, and I tried not to wake her.

What happened at school today? She'd ask if she was awake.

I would tell her Isabelle waved to me today when I sat down in language arts. I would tell her Tae-sung got detention, and I got an A on my *Mockingbird* essay.

I'm worried, I would say. I'd tell her I don't want her to die. That I'm already so alone. That I'd never make it without her.

Honey—she would hold my hand—*tell me something good.*

I would tell her I said hi to the security guard at school. And that he said hi back, how he seemed really happy.

But there was nothing, no words, no breeze.

I lay waiting for the littlest draft to lift the chimes, breathe the hā back into us.

FALL

Prompt: Trust.

I stayed home from school Friday with the worst headache ever. All I could do was binge-watch *Gilmore Girls*.

But Mom figured out that something was wrong. And when she asked me about it, I told her everything.

"You're not annoyed, right? At Noelani?" I asked Brielle when I told her about the lice thing. I didn't want to tell her. She pretty much forced me to.

"Noelani's a birdbrain," Brielle said.

"But you're not mad at her, right?" I asked again. The last thing in the world Noelani could probably deal with on top of having lice was Brielle being mad at her for it.

"First. I. Spent the night. At her house. On Friday. Oh my god, I remember. She was totally scratching. I'm going to have to buy that lice stuff now. And somebody will see me. Never mind, I'll just send the housekeeper."

I wished I could take back telling Brielle about Noelani. Any second, she was going to say something to her. She would say I told. Noelani was so nice. This was going to wreck her.

"Bri," I said, "this is no big thing. Sometimes . . . people . . . just get things."

"WHAT people?" Brielle asked. "I don't get things. I don't get lice. Oh my god, no Branson has EVER had lice. I'm the first one with that crap disease."

"Okay, it's not a disease," I said. This was out of control.

Brielle was pulling drama out of nowhere, breathing shallow and fast. "Noelani backstabbed me. She had me over to her STD house . . ."

"It isn't an STD," I said. "Come on, Bri . . . just . . . be real." I wanted to add that this wasn't about her. But that would've been a waste of air. Everything was about Brielle.

She whipped out the Carnivale list from her binder. The corners were folded over now, and a splotch of green tea smoothie stained the bottom.

I could not be the one responsible for nice Noelani getting Cut. "Come on, Bri," I begged. "Don't Cut her. She's your best friend."

"She kept something from me," Brielle said. "It's over." With her silver Sharpie, she stabbed one angry dot by Noelani's name.

That's what I told Mom. All of it.

She hugged me.

"What can I do now?" I asked her.

She said, "The hard thing is right."

WINTER

Prompt: Have you broken a rule because you thought you had to?

It took a lot to convince Dad. But finally it worked. He told me to drink a lot of water and get some rest. Then he left for work, and he let me stay home.

I just wanted to be with Mom, that was all.

While she slept in, I lay in my bed, listening to Reel Big Fish.

There wasn't a lot to eat. I had a pickle, and I tried to make a mocha, but the coffeepot filled all up with grounds somehow. I thought it would be nice if I baked us something. There was a yellow cake mix, but no eggs, so I added extra water. After the cake baked, it came out flat, and when I poked a fork in the middle to check it, I could tell it was going to be all crumbly.

I thought maybe frosting could fix it all. We didn't have powdered sugar, but we did have the regular kind, which I mixed with a package of hot chocolate. There was a corner of butter in scraggly wax paper, and I added it to the sugar and powder.

I served up two big pieces of crumbly cake, runny frosting for Mom, and we sat under her quilt and ate it, and she told me it was the best cake she'd ever had.

FALL

Prompt: Awkward.

During math, Noelani was washing her hands in the bathroom, staring at her new self in the mirror. I didn't know what to do. What was the hard thing? Telling her I was sorry? She didn't seem like she wanted to hear that.

Noelani grabbed a paper towel. "You didn't have to tell her." She left.

People are saying Noelani and her sister had super lice that wouldn't die, that especially Malea lost a lot of blood to the bugs. Someone said they had to take suppositories. When they came back, both of them had completely new dos—bangs and a bob for Noelani and a pixie cut for Malea.

Things will blow over for Noelani and Malea. They'll get past this. They have each other.

Yesterday I asked Brielle again what she was doing for Halloween, and she said she's thinking about going to the Haunted Lagoon up at the Polynesian Cultural Center. I asked Dad if I could go to the Haunted Lagoon, too, but he said Kamehameha is not a good road.

I told Dad there's a canoe ride and the Laie Lady ghost. I told him how Li Lu and I have spent ALL our Halloweens on Waikiki. Dad said we've only been here for two so far.

Also, I still can't find my iPod cord. I KNOW Eli took it. I looked in the freezer again, all around the berries and cartons of ice cream and Eli's pizzas and tater tots that are spilled out all over.

He sat at the table, watching me, laughing. He thinks it's hilarious.

WINTER

Prompt: "Forgiveness is the attribute of the strong." (Mahatma Gandhi, 1869–1948)

After school, I saw Macario with his board tied on top of his old blue Celica, and I asked him if he was going to Bowls, his favorite wave, and he told me he was going to Sunset, which was surprising.

"Can I come?" I asked him.

It was now or never, going back to where it had all happened.

Macario wasn't a hundred percent, I could tell. I wonder if he was thinking he didn't want anyone to see him with me, the girl whose brother killed his two friends. Or maybe he thought people would think we were together? He never seemed like the type to care what people thought. He said, "Don't you have homework?"

It was funny. Macario never did homework. Eli, either. Or Koa. Or Tate. They would tell me, "Who gives a rat's *** about homework?" and they'd laugh wildly.

I shook my head. "Please, Mac?" I called him the name Eli always used.

He looked at his Celica and shrugged. "'A'ole pilikia," he said.

Macario drove super slow. It took us an hour to get there. We were listening to Pearl Jam, old-school, and he was probably as glad as I was not to talk about nothing.

I could have closed my eyes, or looked away, but I didn't want to. I wanted to see it. I'd already seen it in my mind a thousand times before.

The tire marks are still on Kamehameha. Time, even rain hasn't washed them away. They go left, then right, then they disappear in the gravely shoulder. There's still a bare patch in the pineapple plants.

"Can we stop at Pipe?" I asked.

He knew why. He pulled onto the shoulder across from the Volcom House. A few months back, this place was packed with tents, tarps, banners, bikinis, and trucker hats who came to watch Joel Parkinson take the Triple Crown.

The path opened up to the once-giant wave that would rest till next winter. At our backs a skinny chicken scratched under a smooth wooden sign—"Not soon forgotten."

It was written in red marker—"Koa Okoto"—scribbled in among Todd Chesser, Mark Foo, Andy Irons—the legends who left way too early.

I didn't want Macario to see me cry. But he didn't care if I saw him. Tears streaked his cheeks. "Ke ola . . . küpina'i . . . ho'i . . ." I could make out "life," "echo," "returns."

We went up the street to Sunset. Sunset, with water so clear, so blue, its froth fizzing up on the golden shore, pulling itself back away. Sunset, where palm fronds rustle louder as the sun's heat shrinks, where 'elepaio birds chirp and lizards scratch along the trunks. Sunset, where the salt rides off the water and comes to you sharp and clean. Sunset, so simple, so rich, real, and whole, it is everything you need, even though you'd forgotten, and you want to cry out how sorry you are.

Hugging my knees to my chest, I pretended to see Eli and Koa and Tate paddling out to the swells, sizing up breaks, slicing through barrels. I was mind-surfing, they'd say, and almost smiled to myself.

Still, I concentrated on the waves—weary this time of year but still blue, then green, then white—rising and folding and rising again. I swear I saw Eli, Koa, and Tate rising and folding with them, throwing shakas.

I swear I saw Tate get caught in the rip, and I listened for the laughs, but the only sounds were the waves trailing each other to shore, the rustling fronds, the ʻelepaio birds.

The trade winds blew gently, sleepy from their surge in December, and I tried to let them fill me with hā.

Cupping his harmonica, Macario began with a six tab, then added another and another. And even though I'd never heard him play the song, I knew it right away.

How many roads must a man walk down before you call him a man?

Macario's fingers waved over the metal. He rocked forward and back, his eyes closed as the drowsy winds carried the sad, slow notes.

Then the notes got shorter, tighter, fast. Macario held his harmonica like it was the last thing he had in this whole world. His head shook as he held the notes longer and stronger, slow and low, hollow, all alone.

This was the last place on earth where Koa and Tate were really alive. Macario missed his friends. I could hear it in his song. I pictured the empty desks in the back row of English 12.

The last notes floated up and out, over Macario and me and the stretch of white and blue.

"What's that song again?" I asked when the last note dissolved in salt and air.

Macario brushed the sand off his pants. "Zimmy," he said. "That's what they called Dylan."

The answer was blowing in the wind.

FALL

Prompt: Was your family affected by Saturday's tsunami evacuation?

The sirens were the worst. Mom and I heard them even though we weren't anywhere near Waikiki. We were over at the Wahiawa Botanical Garden, and it was everything, being with Mom. Away from Brielle.

"Breathe in." Mom's hand pressed against the Rainbow tree, its bark smooth in every color. "The healing property of eucalyptus is really powerful." Mom closed her eyes, looked so pretty, happy, and calm.

After, we went to Costco. But we got lost, because we never go to the Waipahu one, we always go to the one on Alakawa. The GPS kept saying "Rerouting," so we turned around in a high school parking lot.

That. School.

You couldn't even tell it was a school. All those rectangles looked more like . . . an army base, a jail. It was not even really a color, and the red dirt had stained all along the bottom of it. Pool with no water, empty Coke can. The grass was dry, the palms were dying, and there were boards and bars on all the windows. If you were inside and looked through the rusty screens, you'd see a fish market that was all locked up, or the whole family—mom, dad, sisters, little brother—pushing bags of bottles in shopping carts and strollers over the jagged sidewalk.

I thought some ice head was going to kidnap us for ransom. All we had were mangoes and paper towels.

"Is this school even open?" I asked Mom.

She said it was.

Me, I'd be scared to death to show up there every day. There was no gate to keep out the ice heads.

WINTER

Prompt: "In war . . . all are losers."
(Former British Prime Minister Neville Chamberlain, 1869–1940)

"Did you throw out the birds of paradise?" I asked Dad when he came home, dropped down in the green chair, and turned on the TV.

"They were dead," he said.

"So you THREW THEM OUT?" I erupted.

Dad looked at me.

"WHY?" I wailed. I didn't care if Mom heard. I didn't care anymore if the Tanakas heard. "Why would you just throw them away? Just because they were drying up? So, what, they're not worth anything anymore?"

Dad wasn't saying anything. He was sitting there, and I hated seeing him sitting there. I took a quick breath. "And all you care about is the Mars rover?"

Dad turned off the TV.

He had to get it. "This stuff," I said, "Mars rover—it doesn't even matter."

"Why did we even move here?" I started to cry.

If we had just stayed in Oregon, our family would have stayed the same.

"Taylor . . ." Dad said. He wanted to hug me.

"Tell me," I sobbed. "Why did we leave Oregon? Mom planted

those peonies. She never got to see them come up! It's because Eli was failing English, wasn't it?"

Dad had told us about the rainbows, the trumpet fish, that I'd meet new friends. He'd told Eli that coming to Our Lady of Redemption would be a fresh start, that it was a good time to move.

I waited.

"There were . . . a lot of reasons." Dad got up, tugged at his tie, then tossed it over a chair.

Me, I wasn't letting him get away that easy. Just accepting that there were "a lot of reasons" why he took Mom from the peonies, derailed our whole life.

We stood there staring at each other for a few seconds. I wanted to tell him that this whole thing—all of it—was his fault. Eli was failing English, and Dr. John Harper, author of *The Cultural Relevance of Waters*, could not have his kid failing English. So we moved. To O'ahu. Where Eli ruined our lives.

But I said instead: "THERE AREN'T JUST TWO KINDS OF PEOPLE IN THE WORLD!" My voice bounced from wall to wall to wall, and I put my hands over my ears but kept going: "You're a SOCIOLOGY PROFESSOR!!! You should know. There"—I sobbed—"are as many KINDS of people as there are ACTUAL people! People are just people!"

I stood there, heaving, snot running down over my lips.

Through blurry eyes, I watched Dad's head hang. He looked at the floor. "You're right," he said.

But I didn't WANT to be right. I wanted Dad to be right. I wanted him to be the parent and keep everything together.

My nose started bleeding a little, and I wiped it with the back of my hand.

His head still hanging down, Dad said he should have gone with him.

"What?" I asked. "Where? You should have gone with who? Where?"

But Dad didn't answer. He just looked at the floor.

Me, I went out and sifted through the gross garbage till I found all eight stalks of birds of paradise, then put them back in the elephant vase on the table.

The whole time, Mom never got up. She stayed in her bed under the quilt, blinds drawn tight.

I lay down with her. "Mom," I said, "we can go back to the Rainbow tree."

I remembered how happy, how peaceful she had been, her hand on the tree, her eyes closed.

"That would be nice." Mom's words echoed empty.

FALL

Prompt: When have you had to be your bravest self?

The rainbows, Dad was right about those.

But he never said anything about turtles.

We hadn't unpacked all the boxes before Mom took Eli and me to Waikiki for the first time. A rainbow stretched from the edge of the buildings right into the sea, over Eli.

Mom kept calling to him to come back to shore, that he was too far out on his surfboard, and Eli would come in closer, then go back out again.

We were decent swimmers. Mom made us take swim lessons every summer in Oregon so we'd be safe around the rivers and lakes. She didn't have to worry about Waikiki. It's not even real, its sand siphoned from offshore.

"Ankle biters." That's what Eli and Koa and Tate and Macario call the Waikiki waves. It's nothing like the North Shore, where swells pound the shore.

Me, I was jumping over those ankle biters. I was jumping over and over and over.

Every so often, I'd yell out to Mom, "Watch this! Watch me!" And I'd jump under a wave, come up, wave to Mom, and she would wave back to me.

But suddenly, I saw this big dark pointy round thing out there with Eli. I didn't know what it was, but I did know it wanted to eat us. I ran back to Mom.

Shivering in my towel on the shore, I saw that pointy round thing bob up and down out in the water. Once or twice, it even came up above the waves, too.

Mom rubbed my trembling back: "That's a turtle out there," she told me.

I had never known turtles to be that big. We had turtles in Oregon, but they could fit right in your hand. There was no way they could eat you.

Mom and I watched as another pointy round thing joined the first, and two more after that. Their great shells rolled to the top of the water.

"LOOK, MOM! TURTLES!" Eli called out from far away, kicking over to them. He bobbed up and down beside the turtles, waving at us.

I didn't wave back. I couldn't move. Eli was going to get eaten, and Mom and I were going to see it. There was nothing we could do to save him.

"Don't worry," Mom told me, "Eli's okay. Those turtles just want to play. They're called *honu* here, and they're vegetarian."

That didn't stop me from worrying. It made sense that even vegetarians, if they got hungry enough, would go after anything.

It took weeks before I went back in the ocean after the first time seeing the turtles. For a long time, whenever I saw a pointy round head poke through, I'd head straight for shore.

But not Eli. Every time, Eli headed straight toward them.

WINTER

Prompt: Grumpy Cat.

I'll give school everything. I'll get caught up. I'll get it together.
Grumpy Cat

"Check it out, Grom!" Eli's feet were up on the coffee table. He was laughing, showing me his phone—a cat with an upside-down mouth and the word *No*.

"That doesn't make any sense," I told him, and Eli said, "You want to see it again, though, right?"

He held out his phone with the same cat, different word: *Yuck*.

"Look at this one," Eli kept saying. There was an *I hate people* one, *Good, I want to bury you in the grass*. Every meme made him laugh more and more.

"These seriously don't make any sense," I said. "I don't get it."

But Eli just laughed.

He thought that was the funniest thing ever, too.

He's so irresponsible.

The things he's done, they go on and on, and he doesn't care. He isn't here to see it.

* * *

It was worse than ever, the smell yesterday. Like something was rotten, or rotting. I tied up and took out the garbage, looked in the laundry room, checked the microwave. There was nothing.

Later, while I searched the fridge for something to eat, I found the terrible, awful thing.

Pushed against the back on the lowest shelf was a to-go container of some kind of pūpū oozing smelly slime—seaweed or sprouts or mushrooms or something.

I double-bagged the unidentifiable slime and threw it in the can in the garage. Then I went through the rest of the fridge and the freezer, too, tossing out salad dressing, ice packs, a bunch of tater tots that had spilled out of the bag, two taquitos, some hamburger meat that could have been a thousand years old. I threw out the Phish Food and Cherry Garcia.

But I kept the mushroom and olive pizzas. I stacked all four of them on top of each other and put them on a freshly wiped shelf. I pulled out the ice tray, and there it was—my iPod cord.

Cold in my hand, it was probably completely useless now, but I wasn't going to toss it in with the tater tots and the Phish Food, to throw it away like Dad did with the birds of paradise. Instead, I held onto it and thought about Eli, watching me from the table, laughing.

He'd tell me, *No deal, Grom*, when I told him he owed me a new one. He'd say he was doing me a favor, because we'd totally laugh about this when we were older, when I could see how funny it was.

The door to the freezer blew out frozen air, waking me up.

What did Dad mean, that he should have gone with him? He should have gone with him where?

FALL

Prompt: The hurricane.

Mrs. Tanaka says it's hotter these days on O'ahu. She says the trade winds come less and less.

Eli is in big trouble.

OLR called Dad at work, and Dad told them he thought Eli was in school.

What did Eli do, take off his shoes and hit the swells? Um, yes. He totally did.

Mom told Dad, "Just wait first, see what he says . . ."

But Dad had already come home for the day—he had canceled his classes. He cut her off: "I'm not doing this with him, Julia. He can't just do whatever he wants here. We all have responsibilities. You let him slide with that D in English."

"Come on, John," Mom said, "we have to be reasonable. We don't know the details . . ."

"He's slipping here," Dad said. "He should have played basketball. Would have kept him out of trouble . . ."

Enter Eli. "You're home early," he said to Dad.

"How was 'school'?" Dad asked him.

There was one second of terrifying silence, then, out of nowhere,

Dad started in: "Have you been drinking? You smell like a brewery. Who was it, Stacy? Did she buy for you again?"

"What?" Eli said. "She wasn't even with us!"

"'Us'? You and that Koa kid? The one who looks like he's high all the time?" Dad went on.

That really annoyed Eli. "God! Okay, I skipped school—I didn't think it would be the ******* end of the world! NOBODY was drinking! Keep Koa out of it! We just went to Bowls—"

"'Bowls,' yeah, right," Dad interrupted. "'Nobody was drinking,' nobody, huh—" Dad was so mad, Eli's swearing didn't even sink in. "Then why do you smell like it?"

"Calm down, okay? No one was drinking."

Probably, I thought, there was some drinking.

There was a *thunk*, like a chair against the floor.

I prayed the Tanakas wouldn't call the Five-0, who would come and take someone away:

Jesus, please. Keep my family all together. I'll never ask for anything again.

"'Nobody was drinking'?" Dad said again. "You just run into chairs completely sober?"

"I didn't see it! All right? Okay? I can't even think when you're yelling at me. You're way off base. You're out of touch!"

"He thinks I'm off base. He thinks I'm out of touch!" Dad was yelling at Mom. "He skips school and gets hammered . . ."

The front door opened, and Eli's truck started up, then peeled away. And someone dragged the chair back to the table.

WINTER

Prompt: How can eighth graders help conserve natural resources?

Where's Mom???

She's gone.

What did Dad do?

Why won't he tell me?

When is she coming back?

After I came home from school yesterday, she wasn't in bed—she wasn't home. I thought maybe she went to Foodland, or Safeway, or to the nursery, or back to work, but in my bones I knew she didn't, and I called Dad at his office.

"How was school?" He tried to be normal, but I wouldn't let him trick me. "Where's Mom?" I said. It was hard to breathe.

"She's okay, Taylor. She's going to get better."

"What did you do? Where is she?" My loudness scared me. "You threw her out, right, like you did with the flowers?"

Was this the big change? Was this what Dad was talking about doing? What did he do?

"She's with people who will take care of her," Dad said. "She's getting help. I have a late meeting. We can talk about it later."

"Who? Who's helping her?" I was begging him to tell me something, anything. "Why didn't you tell me? Why doesn't anyone tell me anything? Where is she? Dad? When is she coming back?" Snot ran down over my lip.

Was Mom sad, too, wherever she was?

"Did she want to go?" I was shaking. "Did she want to leave us?"

"Taylor," Dad said, "you have to be strong here. Mom wasn't taking care of herself, she wasn't eating . . ."

"She WAS eating!" I burst. "She had hot chocolate cake! And toast! And tea—"

"We'll talk about this later," Dad said again. "Right now, I have a meeting, and you have to pull yourself together."

"You just go right on with your work—"

Dad cut me off. "Pull yourself together. We'll talk about it later." He hung up.

I tried to pull myself together. If I didn't, Dad might send me away, too. I lay on my bed and tried reading *Mockingbird*, but I couldn't remember what I read after I turned the page. I switched to math, but the numbers didn't make any sense.

Where was Mom? I wondered. *Did she miss us?*

It was dark when Dad came home and sat down at the edge of my bed. "Mom is working on getting better," he said. "She's in a nice place."

"What kind of 'nice place'?" I asked. "The same kind as Eli?"

Dad's brow dipped. "The doctors have already helped her a lot."

"When is she coming back?" I asked him. "If the doctors have already helped her, if she's getting better, then she can come home."

"Soon," Dad said.

"WHEN?"

Why isn't he telling me???

"She needs to rest, Taylor. She wasn't well. She couldn't take care of herself. You and I have to get through this. There's pizza, Big Kahuna's."

"Can we see her?"

Dad shook his head. "No visitors for a while."

We sat there, Dad and me.

Then he took in a long breath of air and blew back out. "The best thing for us here is to keep doing what we're doing. Right now that means having dinner."

Having pizza wasn't right. You didn't just eat pizza when your mom got sent away.

I took a sad slice, its cheese all cooled to a solid slab, just to show Dad I had myself together. One by one, he was getting rid of all of us.

I took it to my room, shut the door.

"It's your fault," I whispered.

Almost-Eli smiled down from the wall, his waterproof watch shining in the sun.

WINTER

Prompt: On my mind is . . .

Last night, Dad told me Eli's coming back home for a while. He finished his program.

If Brielle finds out, she'll crucify me. She'll say he has no right to get out, that he deserves to be locked up forever.

"And Mom? Is Mom coming home, too?" I asked.

"Not Mom, yet," Dad told me. "Just Eli, and just for a while, just till he's arraigned." He was standing in my doorway.

"When is MOM coming back?" I asked. "She'll want to see him. And what's 'arraigned'?"

"We don't know about Mom yet," Dad said. "'Arraigned' is court. He'll come back, then he'll probably go away again."

"How long then?"

Dad pinched his eyebrows together. "A long time."

Since that blowup over the birds of paradise, it had been on my mind, what he'd said about Eli. That he'd been too hard on him, that he should have gone.

"You said you should've gone with him," I said. "About Eli, the other night. Where did you mean? Where should you have gone?"

"Waikiki." Dad nodded slowly. Small shoulders, wrinkled eyes, he looked so much older than before.

"The winters were hard on her," Dad murmured. "Months and months and months of rain . . ."

"I got an A on my *Mockingbird* essay," I said.

It used to be exactly the kind of thing he loved hearing. But not this time. This time he nodded, got up, and closed the door behind him.

FALL

Prompt: What are the benefits of gender-segregated schools?

Last night, I was setting the table for dinner when Eli came back from Canoe's. He came straight into the kitchen and took a big drink right out of the faucet.

"Glass," Dad said. "Get a glass. I've told you a thousand times."

Eli wiped his mouth on his arm. "Not thirsty anymore." He was in a bad mood. Maybe he still wasn't over that fight he'd had with Dad. Maybe he wiped out. Maybe the swells were ankle biters. Maybe they were big, and he had to wait. Maybe he missed the Big One.

Eli took the lid off a pot on the stove. "What's there to eat?" he asked the same exact second Dad told him to put the lid back on.

Because Eli lifted the lid before the rice was ready, it was going to be all gummy and gross. But cause and effect was something Eli never got. Especially when it came to the rest of us.

"Why are your eyes so red?" Dad asked, pointing at Eli with a carving knife.

When I looked, I saw it, too. Eli's skin was all splotchy at the temples. Was it about Stacy?

"Was that Koa kid with you, the one with the teeth?" Dad asked.

"Sh . . . no," Eli snapped. He was still wearing his slippers, getting sand all over the floor.

That may or may not have been true, that Eli wasn't with Koa. But

Eli's eyes were definitely red and puffy, and his temples glowed like roses. I set down a fork at Dad's place.

"What happened to that kid's teeth?" Dad asked.

Why was he so obsessed?

"What are we having?" Eli asked back.

"Huli huli," Dad snapped.

"CHICKEN?" Eli raged. "Again? GOD! Does ANYONE around here give a **** about life?!?"

"Watch your mouth," Dad said on his way out to the grill.

Muttering, Eli tore through the freezer, yanked out a mushroom and olive pizza. He put it in the oven, scooped up some gummy rice with a spoon, shoveled it into his mouth. "This definitely needs more time."

Then, his mouth all full of chewy rice, he said, "Hey, Grom, your friend came into the shop again."

"Li Lu?"

"Nah, What's-Her-Nuts, Brittany, Brooklyn . . ."

"You mean Brielle?" I asked.

"Yeah, Brielle, the one with money, she came in before."

Okay, it had been twice now. It was definitely a thing.

"Who was she with? Was she with anybody?"

But Eli just wanted to eat, he said.

"Well, did she SAY anything?" I asked him.

"Dunno," Eli said, drinking out of the faucet AGAIN. "I went on break. What's-Her-Nuts Brianna was gone when I came back."

Okay, maybe Eli had a bad day. But I'd just found out my best friend was into my brother. Vomit.

Gender-segregated schools don't matter.

No one's safe from anyone. Not girls. Not boys. Anything can happen. Any single one of us can go down at any time. We're wired to do what we have to, to make it. We have to do what it takes to make our lives happen. Brielle showed me that.

Last night, the Tribal Council voted Russell off *Survivor*.

No one saw that coming. So. Even the bully doesn't have complete immunity forever.

WINTER

Prompt: What defines "good" art?

The rain didn't stay in Oregon.

It followed us here. It's here right now. We'll never be able to get away from it. No matter where we move, even into the middle of the desert, the rain will be there with us.

Glam. Fashion. What is good art?

Good art means something to people. It makes them feel a certain way. It means something. It matters.

The Mānoa Public Library is bigger now than it was before, with a metal roof and long, rectangular windows. But the shelves are still hungry and thin. Before, I always went to the magazine section. Yesterday, though, I wasn't looking for *Vogue* or *Glamour* or *Elle*.

Auntie Alamea looked at my enormous stack of magazines. "No *Glamour* today? No *People*?"

Auntie Alamea has been working at the Mānoa Public library as long as I've been going there, probably even way longer. She wears long muumuus and red lipstick.

I asked Auntie Alamea which magazine would have a bunny in it. I had thought a bunny would be the hardest one to find. But when Auntie Alamea came back with *Rabbits USA*, it had what I was looking for.

On my way back home, I plucked two ripe avocados from the tree on the path. The bowl by the sink had been empty for so long, and Dad loved avocado. Maybe these would make him feel better.

I flipped through the pages of Mom's *American Journal of Nursing* till I found her: maroon paisley-print crossover scrubs, hair pulled back into a loose ponytail.

It was the most perfect art I had ever seen.

I started the scissors at her white clog.

WINTER

Prompt: If you had a ticket to anywhere, where would you go?

Before, this would have been easy for me. Paris. London. New York City.

Home, Mom would say.

Superbay for Eli. Or J-Bay, Bank Vaults, Cloud 9, Santa Cruz. Wherever he thought the Big One might be.

Write words.

Words are tears.

Slippers. Towel. Shorts. Sand.

Shirt, Chili Peppers.

Towel. Hat.

Quintara. Wax.

Paycheck. Poster. Rash guard.

Bowl.

Spoon and milk stain.

Oakleys. Keys.

Towel. Towel. Towel. Leash.

It was hot in there. Stuffy.

His room didn't look like it belonged to someone who'd been gone a long, long time. It seemed like any second, someone would come back and smooth out the balled-up sheet from the foot of the bed, and pick up the *Surfing* magazine off the floor, and bring the bowl into the kitchen.

The door had been closed for so long.

I had just forgotten what it looked like inside. I stood in the doorway, looking at Eli's life.

And there was his computer. I looked behind me, then typed in *sunset* and opened up "Damselfly."

"Perched upon an alien strawberry guava leaf, one of O'ahu's most striking species is among the last one thousand on the island. This year, the endemic blackline Hawaiian damselfly—*pinapinao* in Hawaiian—fluttered to the top of the endangered list. At one to two inches long, the insect is found only in O'ahu's high rain forest, along its cleanest streams, its rainbow eyes reflecting the hypocrisy of hope and promise."

It went on for two pages—about life cycle, then habitat, then how that habitat has been ruined by climate change, wild pigs, mosquitofish. "There are only one thousand left of this magnificent, endemic species. The base of the food chain, when these one thousand vanish, other species will be affected: birds that feed on them, frogs, and fish. And the effects on those species will affect other species, too: larger birds, turtles, even whales, the largest creatures in the sea. All due to the disappearance of one species of damselfly. One incident leads to another and another, a ripple effect that can't be stopped. Every species affects another in powerful, irreversible ways."

I felt like laughing. Eli didn't know anything about cause and effect.

I read on. If he were admitted to UC Santa Cruz's Ecology and Evolution program, Eli wrote, he would work toward protecting the delicate damselfly, fulfilling the hope and promise in its eyes.

He thanked the admissions selection committee for reading.

When Eli comes back, he should clean up his room.

WINTER

Prompt: Today is the anniversary of the Fukushima nuclear plant failure.

Miss Wilson wants us to remember.

She wants our memories to be words, or maybe our words to be memories.

Sometimes those memories are hard to harvest. Sometimes they're hard to erase.

When the Fukushima plant . . . exploded. *Exploded*. Is that the right word? . . . All our moms were terrified the radiation was coming to Hawaii. The news was scary. At best, the poison would wipe us all out. At worst, it would boil our skin and make our eyes pop and our heads bald, and we'd grow third arms and turn into cannibals. Mom made Eli and me swallow iodine pills. We stopped buying fish for a while and ate tofu instead. Eli was happy about that. Dad, not so much.

Now that I'm older, I think about those Japanese kids, how they lost their parents and brothers and homes and schools. Half the people here on O'ahu are at least part Japanese. We learned that in Hawaiian Studies. Hawaii and Japan have a connection.

Eli and me, we used to have a connection with the Tanakas.

They must know Mom's gone. They must wonder where she is. They don't see her watering the lettuce.

All the other New Years, the Tanakas always gave Eli and me *otoshidama*—red *pochibukuro* with a twenty-dollar bill inside each. This year, I know the Tanakas celebrated New Year's. Beethoven played from their house, like it had every other January 1, and I could smell the fish cakes frying. And like on every other New Year's, the *kadomatsu* was outside their door, decorated with flowers and straw. But this year, the Tanakas didn't give us *otoshidama*.

That's something else Eli wrecked.

"Are you okay?" Isabelle asked me today.

I wanted to think of something to say back. But I couldn't. I just stared at her.

And Isabelle softly nodded.

FALL

Prompt: Should Hawaii raise the minimum wage?

They're all over Instagram, both of them—Brielle and Soo—their selfies on the helicopter pad. They're strapped into seats with their helmets on, matching aviators, throwing shaka over the Haiku Stairs. There's a shot of the cockpit controls. Aerials of Sacred Falls. A bird's-eye pic of Punchbowl.

It's everywhere, the helicopter ride Brielle and Soo took together. On Halloween.

i didnt know you guys were doing that, I texted Brielle that night.

How did they do that without me? It would have made all the difference to my whole entire life.

Me, I ended up just staying home. No one in my group had texted me back. And I could never ask Li Lu, not after that big text fight. She'd tell me I already chose Brielle over her. That it was permanent.

I thought I'd just pass out the little chocolate earth balls Mom got from Kokua Market. But no one came over. No one trick-or-treats anymore. Their parents are afraid they'll get hit by cars.

I had ALWAYS wanted to go on a helicopter ride. I was afraid for sure, because of what happened to Grandpa Olie's military company. He survived it, and I would, too, if I had my group with me. I was pretty sure I'd told Brielle that forever ago.

What, the chopper? Brielle texted back a while later.

Yeah, I texted, *i would have gone.*

It was last minute, Brielle texted.

So?

There was nothing for a long, long time. I tried to take my mind off it, flipped between *The Voice* and the Country Music Awards (to see who was wearing who on the red carpet).

Then Brielle: *u dont have the $$$.*

It felt like she had punched me in the stomach.

Brielle has no idea how to be someone's friend. You don't just do something your friend always wanted—NEEDED—to do, without her, without even asking, then tell her she didn't have the money.

Honestly, it's getting old. Maybe I don't want to be friends with Brielle anymore.

But who else is there right now? She's the one with the group. Without her, I don't have anyone.

WINTER

Prompt: Answers.

"Hey, Grom."

That was the first thing Eli said to me after all this time.

I came home from school, and there he was—no shirt, drinking straight out of the kitchen faucet, like Dad had told him not to do a thousand times.

From the salt that had stung his cheeks red, I knew he'd already been out.

"Where'd you go?" was the first thing I said to him, and when he didn't answer, I said for him, "Sunset."

Eli had gotten out, and he'd gone straight to the North Shore.

Then I said, "Was Macario with you?"

I could tell he was, and I told myself there was no reason at all to think Mac and me were friends, just because we went to Sunset that one day.

"And the guys from Ke Nui?"

Yep, even those guys were there. The whole group just took him right back in. After everything.

Nothing had changed for Eli—not his priorities, not his friends. But he had changed my whole life.

"Did they visit you? In there?" I asked.

There was a frozen pizza cooking in the oven. Pepperoni. My kind.

Eli had left the box out on the counter, by the blue envelope, yellow letters—CONGRATULATIONS—open at the top.

Eli wiped his mouth with his arm. "Yeah," he said.

His skin was paler and his hair was darker. A shadow of the seat belt was across his chest.

A fly buzzed at the window, and Eli grabbed the Windex, sending the bug spinning down to the sill.

Suddenly, I didn't want to be all alone with Eli. I was afraid what I would do to him. What I might say. I didn't know him anymore, and I didn't know myself, either.

"Where's Dad?" I asked.

Eli shrugged.

Over the past few months, I had wondered so many things—what Eli had in there for dinner, what he did all those hours inside, was anyone with him, did he ever go out.

I wondered if he was fixed now. If he was sorry for what he did. To Koa and Tate. To us.

Was he still going to Santa Cruz? Was he even going to graduate?

But that's what I wondered before. Before Eli got out and went straight to the swells with his jabronies, came home and drank out of the faucet. Before he was standing right in front of me, all pale, Windex running down the glass.

"Mom's not here," I said.

And Eli asked, "What's the deal with your room?"

"You went in my room?" My face was hot.

"What you've got going on there, it's creepy," he said.

"So what's your plan???" My eyes burned.

Eli looked at me. "Well . . . I'm gonna wait till my pizza's done, then I'm gonna wait till it cools off, then I'm gonna eat it."

"You mean MY pizza!" I said. "And why WERE you driving Koa's Jeep?"

But Eli didn't answer.

He took the pizza out of the oven and cut into it with the wheel, and I knew I wouldn't see him again for a really long time.

FALL

Prompt: Standardized testing.

Tae-sung could give a rat's *** about the state tests, that's how Eli would say it. I know Tae-sung doesn't care because I watch him fill in the bubbles without even reading the questions. He's not going to get into a good college. Or get a good job. Or have a good life. He'll be a boy forever. Dad thinks Eli's going to be like that.

We all already know who's going to do how on those tests. The teachers care way more than we do.

Me, I'll do okay on the reading, but I'm already having a panic attack about the math. I guess I can always just choose *C*.

Also, I changed my mind. Maybe there SHOULD be all-girls schools.

I mean, there's so much boy drama here. Soo said Brielle's annoyed because Henley talks to me in language arts. I told Brielle it was nothing, that I knew she was crushing on him first, that I'm not into him at all.

"I don't even know him," I said. "All I know is that he has good style."

"So, you noticed," Brielle said.

Apparently, she wants everything I have—first my brother, now the guy I talk to.

Mom told me it would be good if I could be kind to Eli.

"I'm always kind to Eli," I said.

She said, "He's going through some stuff."

"What stuff," I asked. "Stacy stuff?"

"Just stuff," Mom said. She's not going to tell me.

WINTER

Prompt: What do you remember about your elementary school?

Today in Latin, I got a blue slip to see Sister Anne in her office. The box was checked "during this class period," not "at your convenience," so I knew it wasn't good. While Miss Wilson passed out the note-books, I stared at that little blue slip. Did Sister know Mom was gone? Gone away in the . . . place? Or was it about my math grade, or my Latin one? Both?

Was I getting kicked out because Grammie didn't want to pay for me to go here anymore?

I'm pretty sure we're running out of money. I heard Dad on the phone: "Could we lose the house?"

What will happen to us then? Where will we live? Would I go to another school? How were we going to eat?

"It's a dress code violation," Sister Anne said.

The old me would have wanted to laugh. The old me would never have violated the dress code.

I looked down at the skirt I had to wear because all the shorts were dirty, and I flattened out the pleats with my palms.

My nails were terrible—red and raw. I tucked them under my thighs so Sister wouldn't see.

When Mom left, the cockroaches came. At first, there was just one. It scurried across the kitchen floor a few nights ago. A couple days later, there were two, then three.

If the cockroaches were coming, the centipedes would be coming, too. And the fire ants would get Mom's lettuce.

I sprinkled borax all around the outside of the house, like I'd seen Mom do. Then I took out the omamori Mrs. Tanaka had given me last summer for watering her cabbage and cucumber while she visited her brother in Japan. It could only be used once, Mrs. Tanaka said about the Ward Away Evil charm, and it had to be used within a year. I had been saving it. Clutching the omamori tightly in my fist, I closed my eyes and whispered, "Please."

"Your skirt is fine," Sister said. "It's the blouse. It's not the standard white."

I tugged at the bow under my neck, like Li Lu had done on Picture Day in the cafeteria.

"It used to be white," I said more to myself than to Sister Anne.

"All it needs is some bleaching," Sister suggested. "Wait here for a minute."

I thought she was going to come back with a bottle of bleach that I'd have to haul around with me, which would be mortifying.

When Sister left, I stood up, looked into the cross-shaped mirror outlined with blue and gold, the scene from Jesus's life at each end. I straightened the big cream bow at my neck and brushed my bangs to the side with my fingers. I could use a haircut and some sun and a little bleach for my shirt.

Of all things, Sister came back with a flyer for the debate team.

"They've barely begun the season," she said. There was plenty of time to join. Our Lady of Redemption had won the state title the last four years in a row. Trying something new would be just the thing, she said.

But arguing about guns and immigration seemed impossible. Even my old self wouldn't have liked that.

"I'm not good at talking in front of people," I told her.

"We have other activities," she said. "Soccer, softball, theater, newspaper . . . I know things have been difficult at home."

I didn't want to talk about home.

"I've been thinking of joining the writing club," I said.

"Very good," Sister said. "The Lord works miracles through the written word."

WINTER

Prompt: Weather.

It's like vog that blows over from the Big Island, fog and ash from the volcanoes, heavy and suffocating and gray. It started with that money stuff, the ache at the base of my head. It isn't pain, exactly. It's more like pressure that wasn't there before. At first, it would be there a second or two, then a minute, then an hour. Now it stays for two or three days straight, and when it comes, I can't do anything to get rid of it. The only thing to do is to lay in bed and wait.

I want to close my eyes and squeeze out all the gray, and never open them up again.

The money. Mom. Eli. It's all about Eli. The same as it's always been. It's always, always been about Eli.

My entire lifetime has been his conferences with teachers and deans about skipping class and missing assignments and not using class time wisely. It's been his trips to the ER for cuts and concussions and the busted shoulder. He's come home late, or forgotten to call, or needs gas money, or his truck got stuck or stolen or broken into.

On bad vog days or bad Eli days, I've laid in my bed under the window, waiting for the trade winds to blow through the curtains, to clean the air and lift the gray.

I've waited and waited, worrying maybe those winds will never come again, that I'll suffocate from the heat and the heaviness, that maybe I'll never see another sunrise.

When those winds do come, when they blow over you so cool and light, whispering promises of hope and change, you feel new and calm at the same time, the simple hā breathing onto and into and all through you. You're alive and whole but also still. It's everything you need.

Lately I've been waiting for those winds a really long time.

And still, everything is somehow moving on. And still, somehow, it's all about Eli, even though Eli's not here.

Dad is always on the phone, talking to banks and lawyers and insurance people.

Does everything have to completely fall apart because of what Eli did? Did he have to take my life down with him? Did he have to wreck my future, when he wrecked his?

In the beginning, I could ignore that vog. I could live with it, pretend it wasn't there.

But that vog inside me, it's grown. It's growing. Maybe I'm dying. Maybe it's a brain tumor, a delayed effect from hitting my eyebrow on the airbag.

If Brielle had even any idea how bad things are, she'd back off. Before we started writing today, she turned around and said, "So, your mom, she's in the hospital now?" Then she just turned back around.

The thing about Brielle is that she doesn't ever back off. She's in it for the long game. I remember that. She won't stop until the vog has swallowed me whole.

I hope she feels like this someday. I hope the vog settles behind her eyes and shuts her off from the world. I hope she can't move, can't talk, can't think, can't exist.

I hope Brielle Branson gets what's coming to her—what she deserves, what she's brought on herself—a hurt so bad she never recovers.

WINTER

Prompt: What does your future look like?

Once, my future was a white T-shirt, gray leggings, aviators, jade flats.

"Dad," I asked him last night, "are we running out of money?"

He said not to worry about that.

But last night I woke up at 3:21 with the vog in my head pressing down heavier than ever. Toast with honey was on my nightstand, the same thing that was on Mom's nightstand before Dad sent her away.

I miss Mom. I miss her so so bad.

When is she coming back? Is she ever coming back?

I thought of those pill bottles on Mom's nightstand. If I took even half of them, I'd never feel any vog again. And even though I knew I wouldn't do it, I know what just thinking it means.

WINTER

Prompt: Dear . . .

Dear Jesus,
I think I'm dying.
Please help.
I'll never ask for anything again. I promise.
XO,
Taylor Harper

I think it's a heart attack.

Last night I woke up at 2:47.

My chest felt like it was being crushed by something heavy and huge, and I couldn't breathe. I wanted to yell out for Mom, but my throat was all closed up. I remembered Mom couldn't help me because she's gone. She was gone, and who knew when she was coming back, if she was ever coming back. I missed her so bad, my whole soul emptied and hollowed, and then the emptiness filled up with ache. Vog pushed down heavier and heavier in my head, then started pushing into my chest, and I laid like that, not able to move, thinking I was dying, praying to Jesus to stop it.

Somehow after, I could move again and got up for water. But I couldn't go back to sleep. I thought the vog would crush me again. I thought about those pills. I was afraid of myself.

For a long time, I had been hoping it wasn't true.

There was one way to know. I got up and clicked the "No" boxes for "I cry often" and "I have become easily agitated." And I checked the "Yes" boxes for "My sleep patterns have changed," "My eating habits have changed," "I have trouble focusing," "I care less about how I look now," and "I would rather be by myself than with friends."

I checked the "Sometimes" boxes for "I feel hopeless." And then there was the worst question. "I have had thoughts of suicide." I paused. Then I checked "Sometimes" for that, too.

I hit SUBMIT, telling myself the quiz would show I had them, the blues.

But the result showed "POSSIBLE depression."

If I was not all the way depressed yet, I wondered, maybe I could fix myself before it actually happened?

Mom would never, ever move forward if something happened to me. I know that for sure, after what happened to Grandpa Olie.

TeenHelp also had "Tips for Feeling Better," and the number one tip was getting outside.

Right then, I got up.

I went out under the stars.

I thought about the wayfinders who sailed from Hawaii to Tahiti with no compass, no map, and only the skies to guide them.

FALL

Prompt: Babies.

When Li Lu and I grew up, we decided, we were never going to have boys.

Boys fight with their dads.

Dad and Eli fight about Stacy.

"ONE TIME," Eli always said. "She bought us beer ONCE."

But Dad won't get over that one time.

Dad said, "She's the reason you're a vegetarian now? You've changed the way you EAT for her?"

"I didn't go vegetarian for her. I've always liked animals, and I don't want to eat them."

"Why doesn't she go to college? What has she been DOING for two years? Working at that earring place in the mall?"

For forever, Stacy worked at Claire's. So I never went in there, even though Claire's had the best feathers and bags.

Instead, I went to Wet Seal, where the feathers fall apart after two days, and the straps break off the purses, and the sunglasses cost two dollars more.

When I really got into fashion, I didn't go to Wet Seal anymore, either. I started going to Macy's, and when I discovered the amazing sale rack, my life became almost perfect. And then, I found Abercrombie.

"She pays her own rent," Eli would say. "She's been on her own. That should count for something."

Dad would shake his head. "I just don't know what you see in her."

Then Eli would say that Dad never, ever tried to get to know her. She's kind, she cares about him, and they have a lot in common.

The whole thing ends with Dad yelling, and Eli storming out, leaving the front door wide open, and Dad pouring a sloe gin and tonic and sinking into the green chair while Mom lies on top of her quilt, and I lie under my curtains, and we both just wait for the trade winds to clear out everything and breathe the hā back in.

This time, though, Mom knelt down in front of him, put her hands on his knees: "He likes her, John. We have to trust him more. You know how it is when parents don't think you're good enough."

WINTER

Prompt: Irony.

Blueberries.

That's the hard part.

But even trying to feel better was actually starting to make me feel better.

TeenHelp's next tip was to exercise. Another was to take certain vitamins and eat certain foods. If I walked to a store, I could check off three things at once.

I made one list for Longs (vitamin B, omega-3, folic acid, Saint John's Wort) and another list for Safeway (blueberries, vegetables, whole grain cereal, eggs).

Blueberries.

They're first on the list of foods that can help with depression. But they're spendy. Ten dollars for a tiny container, imported because of O'ahu's birds.

I wish the best food was bananas or mango or papaya. Those are all over. But it's blueberries, which aren't, so I got a bag of frozen ones.

When Isabelle said hi to me today, I said hi back.

WINTER

Prompt: "No act of kindness, no matter how small, is ever wasted." (Aesop)

TeenHelp said it was important to get up, get out, do stuff.

Yesterday I was in Abercrombie when someone asked if they could help me.

It was Stacy.

The last time we had seen each other was at Eli's birthday at Duke's in the fall.

Stacy was: big bobbly necklace under purple shirtdress with sleeves rolled up, two rings on one hand, dark nails.

"You work here now?" I asked, even though I saw her name tag.

She pulled a top off the rack, turned it around on the hanger, and put it back the other way. "Yeah, I kind of outgrew Claire's." Stacy looked at me. "You're different now. Older."

"I don't really brush my hair now," I said, sweeping it all over one shoulder.

"Can I ring those up for you?" Stacy asked.

"Okay," I said about the white top that wouldn't need bleaching for a while. And the pinwheel bobby pins that just seemed kind of like my old self.

"Have you heard anything from Eli?" Stacy asked.

At first, I was relieved. I was glad that someone asked me about Eli, even if it was Stacy. Someone had said his name out loud.

But then, I realized, Stacy had no idea that Eli had been home. Why hadn't he seen her? Why hadn't he told her he was back?

She took 30 percent off for the "family and friends" discount and handed me the bag. A customer came up to the counter with some high-waisted sailor shorts, asked Stacy to help her find them in size 8.

On my way out, I passed the map. Downstairs. Main entrance. I'd seen that map a billion times.

YOU ARE HERE, it says. It points to the *X* with a red arrow. I saw myself in the reflection—droopy eyelid, long hair, macadamia highlights.

Again, I read the words. YOU ARE HERE.

Here.

At Ala Moana, on O'ahu, in Hawaii. Hawaii, which has quaked, erupted, been infected with rat lungworm and battered by wind. It's been knocked down by hurricanes, invaded by mosquitofish and mongooses, washed away by monsoons, beat down upon by the sun.

I looked at myself in that reflection and felt a little like laughing. "You are here." How was that even possible? Like O'ahu, I was still standing. Surviving. Somehow alive.

And I didn't want macadamia hair anymore.

When I got home, I took the scissors into the bathroom and watched days and weeks and months and years fall onto the counter and into the sink.

WINTER

Prompt: Look back at the entry from November 6. Is this still true today, or has it changed?

Blueberries: Check
Get up and out: Check
Vitamin B: Check
Omega-3: Check
Folic acid: Check
Saint-John's-wort: Check
Try something new:

When I was done snipping, it came out really short.

I swept back the last of my bangs with a pinwheel pin.

After writing the five lines in his notebook, Henley whispered, "You seem different."

"Yeah," I covered my naked neck with my hand, "It's definitely shorter than I meant to go."

But he said he liked it. And I knew he meant it. He opened his copy of *To Kill a Mockingbird*, which had huge crayon scribbles all in it—big pink flowers and crooked rainbows.

Before I started writing, I looked around the room at everyone else writing. And I wondered how one question could be answered by all of us, me and Henley, Tae-sung, Isabelle, Fetua, Elau, Brielle, even? And I wondered what they're all writing about, right now, today. And what they wrote on November 6, what got them through a tough time.

Our answers must be so different, everyone's. Each of our thoughts, our words, our tears comes out on the paper, and they don't say the same thing at all. Even our letters are different—Henley's bursts of broken lead, Isabelle's swirls, and Tae-sung's taps. Brielle's billions of lonely, slanty *I*s, Fetua's blocky alphabet, my big, round jumble that's all smashed together.

On November 6, what saved them? What saved Isabelle?

For me, it was my closet. My closet was there when no one else was.

Is it here for me now?

Or does my notebook save me? Has that changed?

FALL

Prompt: What has helped you through a tough time?

I have a seventh sense for fashion, I told Mom.

And she told me that was really something, to have a seventh sense. Because she said most folks don't even have a SIXTH sense.

"Oh yeah," I said, "I mean that fashion is my sixth sense." I can put things together that wouldn't normally go—just like Tavi Gevinson does. "For example," I told Mom, "I'll pair a coral scarf with a navy-and-white skirt, and it looks amazing. It's called color blocking."

"That's great," Mom said again. She was reading her hospice newsletter.

"I mean," I went on, "can you even imaginc if there weren't people like me and Tavi and Rachel to mix colors and textures and prints in the world? It would be so boring."

"You do have an eye for that stuff," Mom said.

For the billionth time, I wished she would let me give her a makeover, even just a teeny one. I could make her major.

Brielle's mom has great looks. At the fall festival, Mrs. Branson was: low-cut, short black dress, cowboy hat and open toed half-boots, and all different really long chain necklaces. That's what pineapple money can buy you. Mrs. Branson's family goes all the way back to the missionaries. They came and planted pineapple plants, and now Brielle can have anything she could ever want.

Our whole group tells Brielle how amazing her mom dresses, but Brielle says, "Oh my god, it's so embarrassing. She wears the tightest pants in the world. She takes stuff out of my room without even asking."

Our whole group tells Brielle her mom could be her sister. But Brielle says she already has a sister.

Brielle should give Mrs. Branson a break. Maybe her closet is saving her from something.

When I found out about my group going on the helicopter ride without me, I stayed in my room and put together looks—maxis with belts and big '60s earrings, a tank with a long scarf and a bobbly bracelet and flats, my long navy-and-white shirt I refashioned as a dress with an orange necklace I hadn't worn yet.

I had purpose, a future—white T-shirt, gray jeggings, aviators, jade flats.

WINTER

Prompt: Is honesty always the best policy?

Mom's back!

When I came home after school yesterday, her Adele CD was on! She was in her bed, on top of the green-and-white banana-leaf quilt—not under it, which was something. I plopped right down next to her, and her eyes watered up, and she tucked my short hair behind my ear with her thin, slow hand.

"I'm sorry," she told me. "I didn't want to go. I didn't want to be gone that long."

There were five or six pill bottles on her nightstand. Triple what there was before.

"Are you better?" I asked her.

"I'm getting there," she said.

There was no talking for a little while. We just waited for the trade winds. Then Mom said, "We should have gone to San Francisco. For winter break. It was me, I was the one who didn't want to go, and then Eli . . ."

"Mom, it's not your fault," I told her.

It was Eli's fault. That's whose fault this is.

I asked her, "What was it like in there?"

"There was a fishpond," she said quietly. "In the courtyard, with koi."

"That sounds nice," I said.

"Not as nice as this." She smiled a tired smile. "Not as nice as being home." She propped herself up. It took a lot out of her. "How's that eye?" she asked.

It would never be the same. The cut had healed up, but the lid would droop forever. "Oh, it's good," I told her, instead of saying I stopped wearing mascara because I cried it all off every day and who cared how I looked anyway.

"Short hair now," she said.

I didn't want her to worry about my hair, my eye, or me. I didn't want her to think I was making random, impulsive decisions. I didn't want her to worry about anything. I didn't want her to go away again. She had come back this time. But next time, maybe she wouldn't.

Sometimes the truth can hurt more than a lie.

"It's the new thing." I sat up and gave my bangs a little push to the side. "Everybody's doing it, all the celebs." I told her about this year's Oscars looks: Michelle Williams, Gwyneth Paltrow . . .

"Did you watch with Li Lu?"

I told her no.

"How is she?"

There was no way I could tell her I had no idea how Li Lu was. That I had lost my best friend. I thought about how Li Lu probably tossed her "Friends" locket into the waves at Sandys or something when she went with Brielle. I wanted to tell Mom. I wanted to cry. But the hard thing was the right thing. And the right thing was saying, "She's good."

"Whose dress this year?" Mom asked. "The Oscars, whose was your favorite?"

"Viola Davis, definitely." I was suddenly getting a second wind. "Silhouette cut, so long it swirled around her feet."

Mom lay back down. "It sounds lovely. How's school?"

"It's good," I went on. "I'm joining the writing club. It's called Ticket to Write."

"I love your writing." Mom closed her eyes. "They will, too."

I asked Mom if I could make her some toast, but she said no thank you.

"Lilliko'i tea?"

"We're out."

"Green, then?"

Mom shook her head.

"Blueberries!"

They weren't doing much for me yet. Maybe because they're the frozen kind.

Mom closed her eyes and said, "I'm okay."

We were both lying. We were doing it to save each other.

"I'm sorry. I'm so sorry," I whispered, closing the door behind me.

That was the whole entire truth.

WINTER

Prompt: Keeping up.

Blueberries: Check
Get up and out: Check
Vitamin B: Check
Omega-3: Check
Folic acid: Check
Saint-John's-wort: Check
Try something new:

The lying is hard. It's wearing us out.

When Mom got up and went out to water her lettuce yesterday, Dad called up the lawyer. He talked about "vehicular manslaughter," which made me think of butchered cows and chickens and pigs. The "slaughter" part definitely didn't fit with Eli. Eli loved animals.

While Mom watered her lettuce, her ginger, her pink hibiscus, Dad said things like, "Do you think we can get those twelve years down to eight or ten? The kid will be thirty when he gets out." And "Can't we try for some kind of community service?"

He asked, "How much will that end up costing us?" And "How about the jury trial?"

Then the hose turned off. And Dad told the lawyer he had to go.

That whole time, I was making myself a snack. Someone had gone shopping. It wasn't Mom. Mom never bought the strawberries and cream kind of oatmeal that had the sugary white powder and came in individual packets. There was orange juice in actual cartons, too, not in the frozen cans, and there were prepackaged southwest chicken strips, and cinnamon rolls in tubes.

I was mixing up the sugary white powder with the flat oats and the bits of strawberry, and Dad had just put his phone back in his jacket pocket when Mom came back in.

"How's everybody?" she asked.

"Great!" Dad and I said together.

TICKET TO WRITE
DAY 1

Prompt: Describe a place.
Kokua Market

Tomatoes. Potatoes. Peppers. Papaya.

At Kokua Market, where Mom and I go, there are $10 baskets of blueberries.

Bunches of bananas and bunches of kale lay side by side in greens, purples, and reds.

Boxes of lemons and limes, and bins of blue taro to be boiled, peeled, and pounded into poi. We don't make it—it's bitter and bland—but we've had ourselves plenty.

Thin skins of mango—bumps and dots sprinkled over the bleeding oranges and golds. The stems, where the sweetness seeps.

Hanging scale.

Star fruit. $.99 a pound.

Lots of plants, but they aren't for sale.

Bulk takes up one whole aisle—jasmine rice and Bhutanese. Long grain, medium, and short. White and brown, basmati, black. And just as many beans—adzuki, lima, black-eyed, kidney. Chickpeas that look like funny little heads. Northern. Navy. Pinto.

Lentils, too—in shades of soot. Seeds, nuts, grains, dried pineapple.

Pasta. Pretzels.

Coffee. Tea.

Deli—masala, teriyaki.

Meat gets its own room. Chicken, plucked and rinsed and wrapped in plastic: NO ANTIBIOTICS.

Beef—LOCAL!

Snapper. Cod.

Cheese, eggs, milk—almond, soy, coconut, goat.

Rows and rows and rows of yogurt.

Bread so fresh it molds in two days.

Shelves of shampoo, coconut lotion, vitamins—A, B, C, D, E.

Burt's Bees, Rescue Remedy, lavender soap.

Floor—white, scuffed from carts and slippers and skateboards and longboards (when the guy with the glasses isn't looking).

Counter, register, flyers all posted up—UKULELE FESTIVAL, KAPI'OLANI FARMER'S MARKET, COMMUNITY GMO MEETING. SIGN UP FOR OUR NEWSLETTER.

"Are you members?"

We are, Mom and me.

Maui onions—by the door. "Special: $.79."

WINTER

Prompt: On my mind is . . .

Blueberries: Check
Get up and out: Check
Vitamin B: Check
Omega-3: Check
Folic acid: Check
Saint-John's-wort: Check
Try something new: Ticket to Write!

At Ticket to Write, Miss Wilson told us to describe a setting.

I was definitely not expecting to see Henley there. I mean, here in language arts, it takes him all fifteen minutes to get five lines down. Or maybe he writes haiku?

I'm pretty sure he won't be back, though. Because of how the bus doors shut right in his face.

That's not what I told Sister Anne when she called me in to see how it all went.

"It was great," I told Sister. "Miss Wilson put the desks in a circle, and Fetua Tanielu read about giant spiders taking over a human colony on Planet Zithra. The spiders lured humans into their webs with giant TV screens, cell phones, diamond necklaces, and SUVs, and when the humans went to go get those things, the spiders grabbed them and poisoned them and spun them in silk and drained out their blood."

Sister Anne looked terrified, told me I could go back to class.

"Are there any comments?" Miss Wilson had asked after Fetua had read about the spiders.

We were all sitting there in the circle, speechless over Fetua's story.

Fetua wrapped her arms around herself.

Her story was going to make her a billionaire. I could see it as a movie, even. Then I started thinking that maybe joining Ticket to Write wasn't a great idea. I was never going to come up with anything as good as giant spiders trapping greedy people.

Still, no one was saying anything. Fetua wriggled around in her desk. She bit her bottom lip. I could tell she was wishing she could go back and not read that chapter out loud. I could tell she was thinking maybe she wouldn't write any more of it.

"It's really good." I broke our silence. "The symbolism and everything. It's really clever."

"Thanks!" Fetua looked relieved. She wrote some notes on her story.

After that, a few other people read some of their stuff, too. But nothing was as good as Fetua's. Then writing club was over, and Henley walked with me to the bus stop, and he did the thing where he leaned in and his mouth fell open a little, like he was going to say something.

"On some level—" his lips opened, then closed, then opened again, "all of us are completely mortified by our families."

Henley wore really nice shirts with the sleeves rolled up, and had good hair and style, and Brielle Branson was totally in love with him.

How could he be mortified by anything? How could anything in his life possibly be wrong?

"Even mine," Henley went on. "Even my family. Completely, unbelievably mortifying."

"Your mom?" I asked him.

"A little," he said. "But mostly my dad."

"Like how?" I had to know. The most perfect boy in the world was telling me his life wasn't so perfect after all. Did he smell like salami? Have a ton of chest hair or something? Whatever it was, it couldn't be as bad as my situation. As bad as what Eli did. As bad as Mom being sent away. As Dad working all the time, not wanting to be home with us. As Grandpa Olie just giving up.

"Come see," Henley said. "You can come see right now. Come have dinner with us."

Henley Hollingsworth was inviting me to his house. For dinner.

Down Dole Street, the #5 rattled and rumbled, would be here any second.

"You got over me so fast," I said, without thinking. "For the longest time, you didn't text me, you didn't talk to me, I thought you hated me like everyone else . . ."

The bus stopped, and the doors flapped opened.

"Okay." He shrugged, right before they shut in his face. "Maybe another time."

FALL

Prompt: Election results.

Eli's birthday dinner at Duke's: a disaster.

WINTER

Prompt: Letting go.

Grammie came. It was a surprise.

"What's going on here, John?" Her voice was as sharp as Mom's garden shears. She was in the middle of the living room, her hands on her hips. She didn't say hello when I came in from school. Instead, she was blasting Dad with questions: "How long has she been like this?" And "How long has this been going on?" "Why didn't you tell me? I could've come earlier." "This is the reason you couldn't come visit. This is why you couldn't come see me, isn't it?"

Dad was rubbing his lips, his chin. I know what he was doing—he was letting Grammie Stella go off, get it out. There was nothing else he could do. She owned his house, his kids, his wife, his life.

"For Pete's sake, John, that's my daughter in there, in bed." "All those pill bottles!" "What are the doctors telling you?" "Are you getting her help?" "Have you tried anything yet?" "For the love of god, how long has it been since she's SHOWERED?"

"Hi, Grammie," I said.

She held out one of her arms toward me but kept her eyes and hips pointed at Dad.

"And no one tells me," she went on. "I find out because the fruit basket I sent to her work last week gets returned. Does she even work at the hospital anymore? They wouldn't tell me: 'Employee rights,' they said."

Grammie waved her hands in the air, all her gold bracelets crashing down onto one another.

"Happy birthday, honey," she said to me. Then, "My good god, your hair! What is this? What did you do?" And "What in the love of god happened to your EYE?"

Then she said to Dad, "Honestly, John, for Pete's sake, what is going on here?" And "What happened to my Olie, it's happening here, too."

I could tell she didn't even know about Eli. She hadn't mentioned him yet.

"I have to go back to work," Dad said. "Department meeting."

Grammie threw her arms into the air again. "He just goes off to work, just like before. My daughter is lying in a rancid bed, rotting away, my granddaughter's lucky to have her eye, and he has a department meeting. I always knew you were that kind of—"

She stopped suddenly, and we all looked when Mom shuffled in, her head hung, her shoulders stooped.

"My lettuce," she said softly, "it's gone. The fire ants got it."

FALL

Prompt: Redo.

I told Eli that maybe his closet can save him. I can pick him a look, and he'll have a future.

His birthday was so bad.

The day before, the paramedics called Dad at his office to say Eli had hurt his shoulder surfing, that he didn't need to go to the ER, but he did need a ride home from the station at Sunset.

And right as we were leaving for Duke's, OLR called to suspend him for too many tardies in economics.

Then dinner happened.

Even Stacy got there before him, and the first thing Dad said was how he reeked of alcohol, then he made Mom leave with him halfway through his huli huli chicken, when Eli said Tate was giving him a party after, and Dad said "No, it's a school night," and Eli said he was eighteen now and could make his own decisions, and Dad got up and said, "First you show up late, smelling like a brewery, then you tell me you're going out on a school night. I've had it. Do whatever you want." He slapped a twenty on the table for my mango burger and told me, "Take the bus home when you're finished here." But Eli and Macario didn't have any money, so Stacy had to pay for the whole thing, even for Dad's chicken he forgot about, and the only ones who made it to the hula pie part were Macario and me.

There have been other times I thought Dad was going to strangle Eli. Over who used all the hot water, and who knows where all the towels are, and who forgot to put out the garbage on garbage day, and who was supposed to mow the lawn.

Eli's one of those people who just never gets a break.

WINTER

Prompt: How does being in nature inspire you?

After Eli's bad birthday in November, I knew it was on me to make my own birthday happen. I was getting my free Frappuccino at the mall, and right across from me, Stacy sat down. She was: polka dot halter, victory rolls, cat eye, and turquoise nails with dark blue swirls. I had not planned on spending my birthday with anyone. Especially Stacy.

"Happy birthday, Taylor," she said.

"Thanks, how'd you know?" I asked her. I didn't have Facebook or Instagram anymore. There was no point in seeing everyone live their lives when mine was pretty much over.

Stacy said she heard me tell the barista when I handed him my Starbucks card.

"Are you working today?" I asked, my tongue frozen.

"A double," she said. "I'm covering for someone."

Dad could say what he wanted about her, but she was definitely a hard worker.

"Your hair is super brave," Stacy said.

"Eli was home," I blurted for no reason. "Well, he was, but then he went to court, and got convicted, and now he has to go back to court again for sentencing, so he's in—"

Jail. My straw hung in mid–mall air. I couldn't quite say that last part.

Stacy said she knew, she'd heard. "How is he?"

I put the straw back in the cup, moved it so that it scratched circles around the bottom, where the big ice chunks had settled. No one ever asked about Eli, how he was.

"I didn't see him much when he was back," I said. The first and last time was just in the kitchen by the faucet. "But he seemed—mostly—the same as before."

It wasn't fair. Mom had changed, and Dad had changed, and I had changed, but Eli hadn't changed at all. He was exactly the same, drinking out of the kitchen faucet like he always had.

Except.

"He eats meat now," I told Stacy. "He ate my pizza, and Macario and him got a Sausage Supreme from Big Kahuna's. I saw him eating it. Are you sad?"

"About the pizza?"

"About Eli."

Stacy sipped her drink. She left a glossy lip print on the lid, then wiped it away with her turquoise thumb.

"Sure," she said. "Definitely, I'm definitely sad. I loved him—I love him still. But things change."

"Eli hasn't changed," I said again. "Except for the meat. He's the same."

"He's changed," Stacy said. "There's no way he hasn't. For one thing, he must really miss Koa and Tate. He must be lost without them."

I had never thought about Eli missing his brahs. Why had I never thought about it before? Eli had lost his two best friends.

Me, I lost Li Lu. I knew how much that wrecked a person.

"He doesn't want you to see he's changed." Stacy checked her phone for the time. "He knows he's made things bad enough."

"You've talked to him about that?" I asked, surprised.

"No, I haven't talked to him at all."

The way she said it, I could tell they were over. Did he end it, or did she?

"But I know him," Stacy said.

Then, "What have you been doing?"

And of all things, I told her I joined the writing club.

"That sounds nice." Stacy said it like she meant it. "I always wished I was a better writer. Maybe things would have been different."

I asked her what she had been doing. She straightened her name tag and said she'd been working, saving up for beauty school to do nails or maybe massage, somewhere off the island, in California or Minnesota.

Stacy had a plan. She had a future.

She dropped her phone back into her bag—mustard-colored, brown-and-black strap.

"That's a good bag," I told her.

"Give me your phone for a sec?" Stacy said.

I slid it over, and she tapped in her number, and smiled: "If there's ever anything you need."

I kept it.

If I ever made it through this, if all I needed to complete my life was the Victoria Beckham tote in citrus, I would need a credit card.

FALL

***Prompt: In the spirit of Veterans Day, write what you think about when you hear the word* veteran.**

Grandpa Olie was the only one who lived when his company's helicopter got shot down in Vietnam.

And even though it was all too much for him to carry in the end, at first he was making it. When I think of the word *veteran*, I think about survival.

WINTER

Prompt: First . . . Then . . .

It all changes so fast. That's the thing that stays the same.

First, I was friends with Li Lu. In sixth grade, I told her I liked Kevin Loo. He wore tight, bright polo shirts and smelled like bologna. She knew Dad and Eli fought all the time.

Then I was friends with Brielle. It started last year, at the end of seventh grade. We had Hawaiian studies together, and we had a lot of time to talk between arts and crafts and practicing "Aloha 'Oe" on our ukes for May Day. Even though Isabelle and I weren't really on Brielle's level—she lived in Kahala and wore Marc Jacobs and Jimmy Choo, and her mom drove a convertible BMW—I guess Isabelle and I were more on her level than Fetua Tanielu was.

One thing Brielle loved to talk about was why I was friends with Li Lu. She was obsessed. She didn't get it.

"She's so straight-up boring," she would tell me while we wove and printed and strummed. "What is even kind of interesting about her?"

"I don't know," I would say. "I mean, yeah, maybe she's boring, but we've been friends since sixth grade. We know everything about each other."

"No one EVER knows EVERYTHING about someone," Brielle said.

"Seriously, we tell each other everything," I said.

But Brielle wasn't buying it. "EVERYONE has secrets."

Maybe she didn't get Li Lu and me, because now that I think about it she definitely cycled through her friends a lot. In seventh grade alone, she was friends with Jasmine Fukasawa, then Isabelle. This year, she was besties with Noelani, then with me.

"You could totally be in the popular group, if you wanted to," Brielle had told me at the end of last year.

At first, I didn't believe that. I wasn't from Diamond Head or Kahala.

"Your brother is definitely hot," Brielle said, "and you're pretty interesting."

I had thought that was such a compliment.

FALL

Prompt: The U.S. Chamber of Commerce reported that teens claim it is harder to be a young adult today than ever before.

It's about information.

And it's not always good.

It can be seeing your group go on a helicopter ride without you. I needed that ride. It mattered to me more than they'll ever know.

Being a kid today is about surviving. Sometimes people you love get hurt along the way.

From the start, I had been Team Kristen. She was eliminated pretty early on, but she came back for Last Chance Kitchen! The whole time, I wanted her to win, because if she did, she'd go back to Korea to meet her birth parents.

But the competition's fierce.

Even though Brooke was afraid of everything—helicopters, which is completely understandable, and heights—she didn't want to pass that on to her son. I could tell how scared she was that he'd be like her. She wanted to win to show him she was strong.

Brooke and Kristen were besties. There were rumors that they were together.

But there could only be one winner.

That's what's hard about now. About being a young adult, I guess.

There's less spots, but more competition, and social media puts a huge magnifying glass on it all. Plus, the ice caps are melting, and polar bears are drowning because of it.

Young adults today, we want to be happy, we want everyone to be happy, to be equal. In the end, it would be great if Kristen and Brooke could both win. But that isn't how it is.

Even the *Top Chef* judges are harsher than they used to be. They sent Jeffrey home for barely overcooked fish. And he was such a nice guy.

WINTER

Prompt: Progress.

On the *Top Chef* season finale, Kristen broke the tie with celery soup. I wanted her to win from the very beginning. She could find her family now. But Brooke had lost. She was sad, I could tell. And even though Kristen was happy she won, she was sad for Brooke, too.

After school yesterday, I was taking the #5 to the Mānoa Public Library to look for Grandpa Olie.

When we had gone two stops, we passed by Bamboo, where Brielle—who had told me for a whole year straight how boring and bossy and plain Li Lu is—was arm in arm with her, my two ex-best friends, together.

Wasn't Li Lu smarter than that? Didn't she know Brielle used people?

What if Brielle brought Li Lu into the Next Cut? If Li Lu got Cut, she'd be wrecked. Seriously. She couldn't even handle getting an A- on a Latin test.

It was horrible, watching out the window. Like seeing a ship steer straight into a reef before it actually happened.

And Soo was right behind the two of them, the three of their skirts all swishing together along on the sidewalk, then cramming all together through the door. They were going to have the spider roll, and they were going to sit in there together, laughing and talking. Talking about people like me.

Was Li Lu going to tell them I liked Kevin Loo in sixth grade, that Dad and Eli fight all the time? Had she told them all already?

The rest of the week, even into the next one, Li Lu and Brielle and Soo would laugh more about how they laughed at Bamboo, about all the funny things that had happened there.

And me, I was on the #5, with glass and metal and pavement and betel nut spit between those girls and me, but really, I was far away, miles and miles and miles away, squeezed out of everything, and I wanted to be a part of it so, so badly. I wanted to laugh and talk with them over spider roll and mango passion fruit tea—now, and again a week from now, and every week for forever. And I hated myself for wanting that.

I hated myself for wanting them to let me be a part of it, a part of them.

I remember how it was having the group.

And now I'm out of it, which is worse because I know how good being inside was. It would have been better never to know that.

It would have been better to never have been inside at all.

FALL

Prompt: Binaries.

I found it, my look for the party at Ehukai. White gauze top, peasant, tassels.

Grammie Stella got me that.

She came to take us holiday shopping, like she had at the end of every fall, no matter where we lived.

Finally, Eli got out of bed. "How's my handsome grandbaby?" Grammie Stella asked him.

I was waiting and waiting for Eli to get up.

In two weeks, we'll be on Winter Break, and he can sleep in every day if he wants.

We were supposed to go shopping, though, and I was waiting forever, and the stores were getting crowded, and all the good stuff was going to be gone, and Grammie was only going to be here for the weekend, and it was taking forever for Eli to get up, and when he finally did, he said he didn't want to come.

Seriously, he's been so completely moody. He sleeps in later than I do now. A big swell is coming, and he's not even kind of excited about catching it.

Grammie hugged him, tucked his hair behind his ear.

"No code against long hair?" Grammie said to Dad, her eyes

narrowed. "For the $22,000 a year they charge me, you'd think they'd have a few rules."

Twenty-two thousand dollars. That's how much OLR costs a year?

Twenty-two thousand dollars x Eli and me + haircuts + Christmas bikes + frozen pizzas and a Mānoa house seemed so much more than Dad and Mom could ever possibly make.

Dad rubbed his forehead, then shifted in the green chair. "We're grateful, Stella," he said, but he didn't seem grateful.

Grammie asked Eli, "Can we pick you up some things? How are you doing with uniforms? Shoes?"

I was going to tell Grammie I needed new shirts and shorts really bad, and probably a skirt, too, and definitely shoes—Steve Madden charcoal half-boots with side zippers and a chunky heel—but Dad said quickly, "They're fine, Stella, thanks."

"How about a few shirts?" Grammie tugged at both shoulders of Eli's Chili Peppers T-shirt.

"He's fine, Stella," Dad said again.

Grammie sucked in a breath, patted Eli's shoulders with her taupe gel nails. "Okay," she said, not really to Dad or to anyone.

She and I went to Ala Moana—to Macy's and Bebe and Anthropologie.

We didn't go in Miu Miu. And I told Grammie about the Victoria Beckham tote in citrus, because I thought there was a chance she'd understand that it would complete my life and get it for me.

But she told me $860 was too much for a tote. That being an independent woman means making and spending your own money. That there is nothing in life more rewarding.

FALL

Prompt: Why is it important to honor privacy?

Brielle read everything.

And I don't care if it takes me the rest of forever, I'll come up with a way to show her how it feels.

My notebook went missing. Miss Wilson met me at the door before class and told me it was just . . . gone.

For days, I've been sick about it all. I've been asking myself if someone was reading it. Knowing all my everything? Spreading it all over everywhere? What was going to happen?

I've been terrified, googling my name every five seconds for hate pages dedicated to ruining my existence. I've tried to remember everything I wrote—anything at all that could completely wreck me for the rest of my life.

Miss Wilson didn't get how it could have happened. She had picked up the notebook after class. She remembered because as she stacked it, she thought how much writing I've been doing so far this year—more than she'd expected from an eighth grader—and that at this rate, she'd probably have to give me a new notebook before school ended in June.

"What happened to it?" I asked Miss Wilson. I was panicking.

"It must've gone missing the period after yours," Miss Wilson said. "Sixth."

She handed me a tissue, said she was so sorry, and asked if I could do vocabulary sheets till the notebook turned up.

That's what I've been doing this whole time. I will never, ever, ever do another vocab sheet again.

And now we all have this prompt. "Privacy."

There's no such thing to Brielle.

She's been acting so normal. All these days my notebook's been missing, I had had lunch with her and Soo. There was nothing even kind of unusual. I told myself there was no way Brielle took it. She said she would never do that.

And she wasn't lying.

She read my notebook. But she didn't *take* it.

We're back together, my notebook and me. It's all bent out of shape, but the words are here. The security guard found it in the courtyard trash can.

Who was in language arts, sixth period, who spent all their time out in the courtyard?

Soo.

WINTER

Prompt: Do you support the proposed railway system in Honolulu?

"I miss you." Li Lu sprinted onto the #5 after school and sat right down. "This is pointless," she said, like she had in sixth grade, when we got in the fight about Jasmine Fukasawa and had malasadas after.

But me, I was caught off guard. It was unforgivable, how she bailed on me like everyone else did when Koa and Tate died. And also ashamed over the terrible stuff I had thought and written. I tried not to cry.

"Why isn't your mom picking you up?" I asked.

Li Lu said she told her mom she was staying for math lab.

"Do you want to go get noodles?" she asked me.

"I can't," I said. I had to go home and make Mom toast and tea. "What, your mom is letting you take public transportation again now? Is she letting you drive in people's cars again, too?"

"You don't have to be mean about it," Li Lu snapped. "A lot of parents are more careful now about . . ."

She stopped there.

"Well, congratulations on your reinstated bus rights," I went on. "Maybe next, she'll let you go to Waikiki."

I knew I shouldn't keep going, but I did. "Brielle, really? YOU are friends with Brielle Branson now?"

Li Lu ALWAYS said Brielle used people. That she was mean and fake and into herself and thought she was better than everyone else.

"Where's your locket?" I asked her.

"Where's yours?" she asked back.

"I don't have it," I said. "It was so seventh grade."

"What are you doing?" Li Lu asked. "Seriously, what are you DOING?"

She could be so dramatic.

"What are you talking about?" I tried to blow it off.

"You aren't DOING anything," Li Lu said. "You're, like, just waiting for your whole life to happen."

She didn't know anything.

"You always say how you're making your life happen," Li Lu went on, "but you literally don't do anything. You just let your life happen to you. You're pushing everyone away, you're just so stuck, and you're keeping yourself there. You're acting like you blame yourself or something. And I know you better than anyone. I know about you. You really don't. You totally don't blame yourself, you totally blame—"

I cut her off. I would show her how I absolutely was not just letting my life happen to me, waiting for it to happen. "Did she give you that?" I pointed at the big silver-and-turquoise ring Li Lu wore on her index finger. It had Brielle all over it.

"It's better than having nobody," Li Lu said. She got up and went to the back.

WINTER

Prompt: How has your writing changed this year?

Li Lu never knows what she's talking about.

I'm not just letting life happen. I'm not pushing everyone away. I'm not stuck.

How would she even know?

In the beginning, back in September, my letters and words started out all round and jumbled and smashed together. But they're smaller now, those letters and words. They're smaller, straighter, more spread out.

Also.

Fetua.

Probably, Fetua hasn't changed. It's more like what I know about her has.

I went to Bamboo by myself. I couldn't get it out of my mind, seeing my old group all going in together. And I didn't want to have noodles with Li Lu. And nobody makes dinner anymore. So I went and got the #4. And I was halfway through it when Fetua came over to my table with a pitcher and asked if I wanted more water. She was: apron with black brushstroke stalks of bamboo crossed together and black pants.

Fetua said she loved my Kokua Market piece from Ticket to Write. She said it was descriptive and accessible. That it had life.

"Are you still going?" I asked her.

She shook her head. "Don't have bus money."

But the bus was just a dollar.

I asked her, "So you aren't going to OLR anymore?"

Fetua rested the water pitcher against her hip. She said she was just working now. That she might go back to school sometime, though.

"You mean, you aren't going to any school?" I asked. "You're allowed to have a job instead of going to school?"

"Eighteen hours a week." Fetua topped off my water and added, "That's the legal amount, anyway."

I thought how she didn't have to deal with Brielle and math and homework. "Geez, you're lucky," I said.

But the way Fetua's eyes dropped, I could see she didn't feel lucky at all. She wanted to go to school. And she couldn't. She was pouring water and wiping tables so her family could have food, electricity, a place to live. Nothing about her life had probably ever been lucky in any way.

I looked down at my #4. The tempura had wilted at the ends.

"Have you been writing?" I asked.

Fetua's eyes lifted.

She told me about her new story—about a government that's banned salad dressing from all women, so the women stockpile it right under their husbands' noses and secretly teach their daughters how to make it.

I'd never heard of anything like that. Maybe the *E* by Fetua's name on the OLR X-Posed page was for *Exceptional* or *Extraordinary*.

I asked Fetua how she came up with that stuff.

Why hadn't I tried to be friends with her before? She was so easy to talk to, imaginative, inspiring. She was moving forward, even though her life was really hard. How was that happening?

But she just said, "You can call me Fettie." That's what her family calls her.

She said to let her know if I needed a box. Then she went to wipe a table in front.

Me, I wiped down my own table. I picked up every sticky grain of rice and stacked up my bento box, napkin, cup, and chopsticks. I left it all in the neatest pile I possibly could near the edge, and shined up the whole thing with a napkin, which I placed on top.

In a month or two, I'd come back. I'd get the #4 again, and ask Fettie how the salad dressing story was coming along, if the people found a way to overthrow the government.

FALL

Prompt: Natural disasters.

Earthquake, tsunami, flood, crash, the Cut.

But I know the Cut is just the beginning. Like the first rumbles of Kīlauea, before the magma bursts.

How bad is the fallout going to be? That's what I've been wondering. Not whether or not it's coming.

It isn't because she thinks I backstabbed her, when I wrote how I wished I'd told Sister Anne she had the tuition list. It isn't because I never wanted to play the Next Cut, that I only half-looked for dirt on Noelani.

It isn't even because I saw Brielle for what she really is—as empty, as selfish, as desperate as the rest of us. It's not that I wrote that she makes EVERYTHING about her. Or when I put it into actual words, permanent record, forever, that she has no idea how to be someone's friend, that she's mean, that she uses people.

Somehow it's not about any of that.

All week, Soo's been acting like nothing has happened. And technically, as far as she is concerned, nothing really has—there's nothing in these pages that throws her under the bus. And Brielle's been acting completely normal, too. Which is terrifying. I think that's the point. If there's one thing she has, Brielle said herself, it's playing the long game.

How long would she keep a lid on all the drama?

It must have been everything to her, how obsessed I was with her life, how desperate I was to be part of it, how pathetic I made myself to get on the Carnivale list.

She must've LOVED how spineless I was. How I let her talk me into playing the Next Cut. How I picked her over Li Lu. It must have kept her entertained for at least five seconds.

There's nothing I can do now to get ready for the wreckage, to prepare—no emergency exit, no food supply, no taped-up windows, no seat belt.

It was phase one, right before language arts today. She turned around. "You're totally Cut. You know that, right?" Her eyes narrowed. "You brought my family into this."

WINTER

Prompt: Polls show America is more polarized now than ever before.

There are two kinds of voters, Dad would say—liberals and conservatives.

But it doesn't make sense to worry about that if you're dying part by part, cell by cell, if your mom has to leave her dirt forever.

In the fall, for history homework, we had to watch the debate. Gun control, immigration, ice caps, jobs, oil, China . . .

Mr. Montalvo showed us CNN, which said the Democrats had won. Then he showed us Fox News, which said the Republicans did. No one really knows who wins. It seems to me, from all the fighting, everyone just loses.

Do we have to pick a side? Nobody in Hawaii even votes. We have the lowest voter turnout of all the states, Mr. Montalvo had told us.

It was all so long ago, I can't remember who really won that debate. A thousand things have happened since then. Besides, it didn't matter.

Neither candidate would help us here.

When I got home from school yesterday, Mom was sitting at the kitchen table. Her hands were on the table, but there was nothing else—no mug of lilliko'i tea, no *American Journal of Nursing*, no hospice newsletter. Did she even have a job anymore? Were we going to lose our house because she wasn't working? Was Dad going to kick her out? Or would he leave us? Where would we live?

I sat down with her.

She said, "How was school today?" It took a lot for her to get out those words.

I knew how that was. I put my hand on hers. Her skin was soft now. Not like before, when she had blisters and calluses from gardening, or from washing off sickness and death ten thousand times at work.

"Is that us?" she asked me. "The people stapled up on your wall? Is it Eli, and me, and Grandpa Olie? And Li Lu, too?"

"And Hopper, is that Hopper?" Mom asked about the picture of the bunny Auntie Alamea helped me find in *Rabbits USA*. He was brown and white, medium-sized, with round, black eyes and long, floppy ears.

"Who's the other boy?" She reached up and smoothed my eyebrow. "The one in the nice shirt?"

"That . . . that is Henley," I told her.

FALL

Prompt: Sharp.

Outside, the plumeria and the palms bend backward and forward and backward in the squall.

The trade winds have come, and they are brutal—knocking over trash cans, ripping branches from flame trees, and shaking the monkeypods.

The rains came along with the winds, slapping hibiscus blooms, even mangoes, into puddles, pushing banyan tree leaves through streets, raising up the waves.

I don't even care that I'm the Next Cut.

But of all the things I could have been Cut for, it doesn't make any sense what Brielle's talking about. That I brought her family into it.

I went all through my notebook.

And all there is is just the most insignificant thing, on October 15. It was how her dad wouldn't take her to Australia and what a baby she was being about it.

THAT'S why I was Cut.

Brielle called her own dad a jackhole. And I got Cut for it.

Half of me wants to laugh like the wind in the palms.

It's like *Top Chef*.

You wait and you wait. And then you get Cut. It's kind of a relief, actually, when you're finally told you're out.

The pressure's off.

You pack up your knives and go home, and everyone knows you're a loser.

But at least you're not just waiting anymore.

WINTER

Prompt: Loyalty.

"She gave you something, right?" Isabelle said. "In the beginning?"

Miss Wilson paired us up to do a vocabulary worksheet. We were trying something new, she said. At first, all the blood drained out of my head and through my body and into my feet. I absolutely could not get paired up with Brielle. But the Queen of Everything was gone. Again.

I really hoped I'd get paired up with Henley. But Miss Wilson put him with Tae-sung. It came down to Isabelle and me.

And we were on number one: *taciturn*.

"She gave you a ring, a phone, a lip gloss." Isabelle swirled the definition into the blank.

I couldn't believe it. Isabelle knew about the start of everything with Brielle.

"For me," she went on, "it was a phone. Silver and black, with a turquoise case. She said she was 'trading up'."

I wondered if Isabelle still had that phone, or if Brielle took it back, like she took back All My Purple Life.

"She came over to your house," Isabelle continued, "but she never had you over to hers." Isabelle paused, looked me right in the eyes. Then, "She told you her big secret."

This part sank my stomach. I was sick at how spineless, how desperate I'd been, how special I'd thought I was, how special I'd wanted to be, how I'd thought I'd mattered.

I didn't want to hear the words aloud. But Isabelle said them. "Chance Cameron."

She swirled the definition for *pedantic* onto line 2. "She made you feel like you were part of some big, amazing, mysterious thing. Something important, exclusive . . . And if you were small, insignificant, if your life was little and boring, Brielle Branson was the answer."

Isabelle stopped swirling. "She pretended to let you decide if you were In or Out. Only it wasn't really a choice, because you knew that if you didn't play, even though she never said it, she'd completely ruin your life."

Isabelle had this whole thing exactly right. It was unbelievable, how it had all happened to her, too. And to who else? I looked around the room.

Tae-sung saw me, wiggled his tongue between his fingers. By the time school was out, thanks to him, everyone would hear that Isabelle and I were lesbians together.

I looked at Isabelle. She didn't care. "First I played along," she said. "With the game, with her. I didn't think it was a big deal, I guess. I really didn't think about it at all."

Who had Isabelle been talking to, watching, waiting on? I didn't ask. I was afraid if I asked, she'd stop talking, and I'd never know how the whole thing ended. How it was going to end for me.

"But all of a sudden, I was in pretty deep. And Brielle gave me a challenge, a choice."

It was painfully familiar. "She had something on you," I managed to say.

"Not on me. On Hailey," Isabelle said.

That made sick sense. Brielle was smart. She knew Isabelle didn't care what people thought of her. So she used what mattered to her.

"The challenge, though, there wasn't much on her," Isabelle said. She'd told Brielle there was really nothing to know.

I knew it was Isabelle's best way out. She thought she could save Noelani and Hailey both.

"Except"—Isabelle got quiet—"there was one tiny little stupid thing. And Brielle knew I knew it."

I knew the rest.

"I wouldn't tell her," Isabelle said. "I wouldn't give her the dirt she was looking for. It didn't seem right to ruin someone's life over basically nothing. But then . . ." Isabelle stopped, stared down at the worksheet. "I didn't think she'd really pull off wrecking Hailey."

"So," Isabelle started swirling in the blanks again, "she Cut me. Which was no big deal. But she posted things on Facebook and Instagram about Hailey and me. She told everyone we were together, that we gave each other mono, that Hailey's parents took her out of school and put her in a conversion camp."

It was sickening. Heartbreaking. Horrible. Wrong.

I stared at Isabelle, I couldn't help it. She lost her friend. She missed her, and she felt responsible. She was such a good person, an even better person than I'd thought. Why hadn't I ever tried getting to know her?

Because she would never be friends with someone like me, that's why, someone who's selfish and awful. Isabelle and I had gone through the same exact thing and ended up the same exact way, but she hadn't meant to wreck anyone.

All along, me, I was just trying to save myself.

WINTER

Prompt: There is order within chaos.
(Scientific theory from Edward Lorenz, 1961)

I can't stop thinking about it, about how crafty it was, how clever, how precise. It was deliberate, strategic, smart, mean. How Isabelle was watching Noelani, then I was watching Noelani, and then Soo was watching me, which probably meant that at any second, Li Lu would be watching Soo.

After what Isabelle told me, I put together the Next Cut, the system, how it worked, the long game.

Brielle played people against each other.

Li Lu knew it. She tried to tell me when we had that big text fight. Brielle had some kind of agenda—she was using us. And now she was using Li Lu.

Why, though? What was the reason Brielle worked so hard? I can't come up with it. But one thing's for sure. This has to do with way more than Brielle being bored. It has to do with survival.

"The people closest to us are EXACTLY the ones we shouldn't be one hundred percent sure about," she had whispered that day in September.

Something was going on.

WINTER

Prompt: On my mind is . . .

It took everything I had to ask Isabelle today, "So, how did you move forward?"

Since she survived her life somehow, I was thinking maybe she had tips.

"Volleyball," Isabelle said, opening up her notebook.

She gave volleyball everything. She signed up for the AAU league and practiced almost every day, she stayed after practice and lifted weights. She watched YouTube, read training books, got private lessons on Sundays from the assistant coach at University of Hawai'i . . .

I wished I played volleyball. I wished I had a thing, a group, like Isabelle, Allie, Ellie, Oliana, Halia.

Last summer, Dad told me he'd trade me a day of horseback riding at Kualoa Ranch if I played the whole season. But the shorts were tight, and so were the girls who had played together since fifth grade.

"What are things like with her now?" I asked. "With Brielle?"

"Oh." Isabelle nodded. "She hates me. When you're Cut, you really are Cut."

She swirled the prompt onto the page.

"She turned everyone against you," I said.

But Isabelle said she did that to herself. She cut everyone off, out.

She was sad, she said. She really missed Hailey.

I didn't ask her about her and Hailey, if that whole thing was true. It didn't matter. Losing someone was losing someone.

Did they ever see each other? Or at least talk? I wanted to ask, but it would just make Isabelle empty again. She had moved forward. She had put the Next Cut and Brielle and Hailey's leaving behind her. She racked up points with serves and spikes, was O'ahu's Athlete of the Month.

"Thank you," I told Isabelle, "for. . . . you know . . . talking to me."

Isabelle smiled. "How's your brother?"

I said he was okay.

Miss Wilson reminded us all to use class time wisely.

Isabelle was amazing. She was brave and strong, everything I was not.

All along, I'd missed out on the possibility of knowing her. In the process of trying to get what I thought would be everything, I'd given up what was actually really great.

Isabelle and me, we could've been friends.

FALL

Prompt: Climate change.

The Bransons' party is over. Off. Canceled. Before it even happened.

It doesn't even matter that I was Cut. If I'd stayed on the list, I couldn't have gone anyway.

People are talking about the whole thing. Instead of Carnivale, they say, Brielle and the Bransons are going on a family vacation to Australia. The whole family, the four of them together. "To get away from it all."

I wish my family was like that. Like we went on amazing vacations together.

I'm over Brielle, anyway. The party at Ehukai will be everything—people, music, fire, dancing. I have my look: white gauze top, peasant, tassels.

Yesterday, Dad found out Eli got a ticket on Kamehameha. He was going 42 in a 35. Now the insurance is going up again.

First Eli tried to say it wasn't that fast, barely over the speed limit, that the Five-0 all over are just LOOKING for people to pull over.

Dad said Eli wasn't even supposed to be UP THERE—the time on the ticket was 9:16 on a school night, and he had no idea Eli was even there. Eli tried to say he must've forgotten to let him know.

"That's flat-out irresponsible," Dad said, and Eli said he was tired of hearing about responsibility, and that really got to Dad.

"When are you going to grow up?" Dad asked him.

And Eli said, "You mean when am I going to quit surfing."

Me, I was so glad Mom was at work. This whole thing would have killed her. Sometimes when this happens, she gets in her bed, and I worry that someday she won't get back out of it.

"Okay, then," Dad said. "When are you going to quit surfing and grow up?"

And Eli's face changed. He went from furious to devastated. Heartbroken. Lifeless, even.

"Come out with me," Eli said to Dad in a small voice. "Tomorrow, after school." His eyes started to sparkle. "Just come see what it's about. Waikiki, the waves are ankle biters, you can use my old Quintara."

I looked at Dad, and Dad looked at the floor. I hoped Dad would go. Eli would love it. He was so happy when people came to watch him.

Outside, the trade winds howled and the monkeypods shook, and the rains slapped hibiscus blooms into puddles that have become rivers.

"It's the end of the term." Dad had papers to grade.

And Eli picked up his keys and walked out.

Like always, he left the door open.

WINTER

Henley just opened his notebook and showed me *LEMON CAKE!!!* above a drawing of a cat.

Seriously???!!! I show him back, with a cat face, wild eyes, tongue sticking out.

It's true. We are something, Henley and me.

I was eating a bag of Cheerios at lunch, and just like before, Henley fell out of the sky.

"Hey," he said.

"What are you doing?" I asked, surprised and confused and happy at the same time.

He pointed at my phone. "'Luck Dragon Lady'?"

I gave him an earbud, and after the song, he put his arm around the low part of my back. I closed my eyes. It felt good, like someone had me. Like nothing bad could ever happen if we stayed right there, like that. I didn't move. I thought if I moved, Henley might move, too. So I closed my eyes to remember, in case it all changed back.

And while my eyes were closed, his lips pressed into my lips, just the tiniest bit quivery.

"I can't get you out of my head," he said.

But he wasn't going to kiss me again. Not then, not there, in the OLR cafeteria.

"I'm starving," I said into the bag of Cheerios. "Do you like to get mall chicken after school?"

"Mall chicken?" Henley smiled. "That's the kind of thing I love about you."

Mullet baby Jesus. Henley said "love."

It was noodles!

Henley brought me noodles all the way from Florence. He had wrapped them up in Italian newspaper, tied it together with twine.

At first, from the shape and size of it, I thought maybe it was a T-shirt—I [heart image] ROME, or something. But it rattled inside. It was noodles! In a paper bag, with a long Italian name that started with an *F* and ended with an *E*.

"Bowties!" I said.

"Butterflies," Eli told me.

He waited so long to give them to me, he said, because he wanted to make them for me. For us.

While he boiled the water, I sat at the counter and watched.

"Americans boil pasta too long. And we add too much sauce." He had picked up those facts in Italy.

"Kit Kat!" He scooped up a little black kitty, rubbed her head. "She came in for pasta."

Kit Kat had a torn ear and yellow eyes. She had a half of a gray whisker, and her paws were splotched with bright pink polish.

Henley told Kit Kat it would be a few more minutes, then set her down on the floor.

His dad and stepmom came in with some groceries. His dad was a happy man. Friendly. I couldn't see anything embarrassing about him. He stuck out his hand, "You must be Taylor."

I could feel the red rush up my neck and to my cheeks. Henley's dad knew who I was? Henley had told him about me? What did he say?

"Nice to meet you, Taylor." Henley's stepmom shook my hand, too. Her nails were light pink, and I wasn't sure if I should call her Nisha or Doctor or Doctor Nisha, so I just said it was nice to meet her, too.

"Hennnnleeeyyyy!" A little girl bounced into the kitchen. She crashed into Henley, her Hello Kitty backpack sliding off her shoulder. She tried to pick up Kit Kat, but Kit Kat ran away.

There was a lot going on. Henley's house was so . . . alive.

"This is my friend Taylor," Henley told the girl.

She looked at me, her eyes big and wide. "I like those in your hair," she said.

"They're pinwheels, see?" I took out a bobby pin and blew on it. "I like how you painted your kitty's feet."

"That's Orchid," Henley said while Orchid skipped off.

Henley's stepmom picked up the backpack. "Please call me Nisha."

His dad started unpacking celery and rice and coconut milk and a big bag of Cool Ranch Doritos.

"Orchid's adorable," I told Henley when his dad and stepmom left.

"She's the reason I'm here," Henley said.

"Really?" I said, then tried to backtrack. "I mean, I can totally see why. I just thought you moved here because . . ." I laughed to myself. Or, I thought I laughed to myself, at myself, but I actually laughed out loud.

". . . Because . . ." I thought about all the drama people had stirred up about Henley, and at the same time, I had to, tried to, explain my obvious total, complete lack of stability. "You weren't FORCED to come here? Because you got expelled from school on the mainland for computer hacking?"

"Computer hacking?" Henley stopped stirring. "That's what you heard? Because I heard it was for possession." He laughed, too.

"I personally never believed it . . ." I started but stopped. Henley was real. He would know the truth.

He wiped his eyes with his sleeve: "Hacking," he said. "That's so great! Better than anything I could've ever come up with. Okay, I'll give you the plain, true, uninspired truth. I wanted to get to know my only sister in the world. " Henley shrugged. "People would have known if they had just asked."

And right then, I knew why I'd been thinking Henley didn't seem whole. Why he seemed different. Why I'd thought he was missing something. Because he WAS missing something. He was missing DRAMA. He didn't even watch *Top Chef*!

He was real—one hundred percent real. He knew what mattered—sisters and cats and good pasta—and I wanted to be like that, too.

Henley's stepmom and dad put away the groceries and asked Henley how school was, like normal families did. Like Mom and Dad used to do at our house.

Orchid sat on the stool beside me, spinning a smashed pinwheel she'd found in her room. If my family were this great, I thought, I would never ask for anything the rest of my whole life.

"Okay, Orchid," Henley's dad said. "Let's check out some kittens on YouTube." He meowed.

Orchid meowed, too. She pawed, then bounced out of the kitchen, pinwheel in her mouth.

Nisha asked if she could get us anything before she left for her garden meeting.

"The plots on Mānoa Road?" I asked. I thought she'd be a good friend for Mom. They could work the dirt together, plant ginger starts, talk about trade winds and blight.

"Ala Wai, actually," she said.

"The big one!" I blurted. Then added less loudly, "Some of those plots are two stories."

Nisha laughed. "Yes, they are! But mine's only one. And it's mostly sweet potatoes."

She left, and it was quiet.

The water bubbled up and boiled, and Henley put in the pasta. He set the timer for four minutes and got out a strainer and butter and two bowls.

I sat and Henley stirred, and we smiled at each other.

"Your family," I said. "They're amazing."

The pasta had one more minute.

"My dad, though," Henley said.

"He's great," I told him. I meant it.

"Yeah, he's great—I think that now." Henley looked so good, with his sleeves rolled up like that. "It took a while to realize, though. Did you catch it, his breathing?"

I shook my head. I hadn't noticed anything.

"He breathes so loud," Henley said. "It was horrifying at first. Try going to the movies with him. It's just better to see something like *Inception*, with bomb blasts and explosions, than *127 Hours*, where he whistles through his nasal passages while James Franco is trapped between rocks."

I laughed. We both laughed.

"THAT'S your dad's fatal flaw?" I said. "Loud breathing? My grandpa Olie died from pills and whiskey, and my brother—"

The timer went off.

"It's all the same," Henley said. "We're completely humiliated by the people who match our DNA. It's inevitable."

He drained the bowties, then tipped them back into the pot with some butter.

"My mom," I said. We were telling each other everything. "She's not okay. My dad sent her off somewhere with a koi pond."

"I heard something about that," Henley said. He was honest. "Is she back yet? Is she home now? How's she doing?"

Henley scooped out some noodles into each bowl, put two on a little plate on the floor. Kit Kat shot right back in, licking the plate clean before Henley even sat down at the counter with me. We turned our stools so our knees were touching, then he poked his fork into a bowtie and lifted it to my lips.

But the steam! I could feel it, and I shrunk back from the fork, almost falling off the stool. "I have a cat's tongue!" I cried out louder than I'd intended, covering my mouth.

"What is that? What?" Henley pulled back the fork.

It must've looked ridiculous, my dramatic recoil from a noodle.

"A cat's tongue," I repeated more calmly. "Mrs. Tanaka told me. It's when you can't eat stuff that's too hot. Like a cat."

"A cat's tongue," Henley smiled. "I like it."

He blew gently on the bowtie, then offered it out to me again.

"Hey, Taylor," he said while I let that amazing pasta melt in my mouth. "Can I ask you something?"

It was about the Thing. He asked me what happened.

And I told him.

I told him about Brielle's game, and how Stacy texted, and how Koa was wasted, and how we all left Ehukai together, and how the Jeep swerved then swung off the shoulder and onto its side. I told him about the blood, the bone sticking out of Koa's arm. I told him about the broken glass.

I told him about the noise—the tires crying out on Kamehameha, like they knew how things were going to end up. I told him how Eli's awful scream bounced off the mountains. How the dirt shook when we hit against it that hard—hollow, like we were going to go right through it to the core of Earth, straight to hell itself.

I told him how the crunch of metal was as sharp as the edges it made in one second flat.

How my ears rang and rang, and I wasn't sure if I was alive or dead, and if anyone else was, either.

I told him I saw the ambulance lights, the paramedics, and I knew everything was supposed to be really loud, but instead everything got dead quiet.

And that's where I stopped. At "dead quiet," *dead*, I just sat there.

And a little bit later, Henley said the most perfect thing. "That's awful," he told me. "I'm sorry that happened." And he meant it. He held out another bowtie.

It was so simple—those words, that pasta, this boy.

Our knees still touching, I passed him back the fork.

"Before it all happened," I said, "there was just Brielle, watching me and Eli and Koa and Tate all leave together. She was by the fire, holding a red cup, just . . . watching us. Watching me."

For the first time ever, someone wished they had my life.

FALL

Prompt: North Korea.

Everything is completely unraveling. We are all literally on the edge of the apocalypse.

If Eli ever comes back home, Dad's going to ground him forever. He goes around the house muttering "grow up" and "responsibility" as he pitches towels into the washing machine.

Well, Dad will try to ground Eli, anyway. Probably Eli will just go out again.

That's WWIII on the home front. Here's school.

The fallout. The backlash.

Getting Cut was just the start.

She took a long time to get it just right, Brielle did. But it's perfect, that's for sure.

First, she took back All of My Purple Life—it was almost gone anyway, had old peppermint gum stuck to the outside—then, she told Li Lu everything.

It was the ONE thing I hadn't thought about, the stuff I'd written about Li Lu. I'd been so hung up on what I had in there about Brielle that I didn't think about my ex–best friend.

Li Lu knew Brielle was going to wreck me. She tried to tell me, to save me, and I Cut her.

And Brielle knew Li Lu and I would be wrecked by all the things

I wrote—the unforgettable, unforgiveable things—the meanest words in the world. I'm sick that I wrote them—how ridiculous Li Lu dresses, that she never knows what she's talking about, that she never gets anything, that she's annoying, that she's been in my business forever, that she's boring.

Even if there was a chance for Li Lu and me to work things out after the text fight, Brielle ruined that chance forever.

Today, Li Lu gave me back *Queen of Babble*—I had lent it to her forever ago. She said it was the worst book she's ever read.

WINTER

Prompt: Magic.

Yesterday, after school, I went over to Henley's again. This time he made us grilled cheeses, with mayonnaise on the outside of the bread, which I never even knew was a thing, and it was actually really amazing.

Also, Henley heated us up some tomato soup. He had made it the night before from real tomatoes! We dipped our grilled cheeses into it, and the whole thing together was so, so good. Kit Kat thought so, too. She didn't leave one single drop on her plate.

And after that, Henley said he had something.

"We're, like, nine months off." He handed me a paper lantern. "Or three, depending on whether you count forward or back. Which way do you count?" He smiled. "Forward! Definitely forward. I remember about you and those look-backs."

"A lantern?" I said. It was lovely. Light. It crinkled in my hands.

"*Krathong*," Henley told me. "For *Yi Peng*."

"What is that?"

"A festival. In Thailand. When we did it here, we had one lantern left over. I thought you could use it."

We went outside on the deck, above the hibiscus and under the palms. A little breeze lifted the fern fronds, and a lizard skittered away across the rail. The sun was pinks and oranges melting together far away. All of it was so perfect, and I wanted to remember every color, every word, the warm Henley's shoulders made against mine.

"What do you think it's like?" Henley asked. "For Eli? In there?"

"He can't surf," I said without even thinking about it.

"That's rough," Henley said with surprising empathy.

"You surf?" I whirled around and looked right at him. Because if he surfed, this whole thing was totally and completely off. I was over surfers, all of them.

Henley laughed. "Never tried. You?"

I told him, "Nope. No way. Nuh-uh."

"But you know how it is not to be able to do what you love," Henley added so honestly.

I thought about how much I've missed watching *Gossip Girl* and reading *People* at Li Lu's, and sneaking off to Waikiki with her, and getting manis at Paul Mitchell. I missed going to the farmer's market, even to Foodland, with Mom. How much I missed driving to school with Eli. How much I missed seeing Koa and Tate around. How much I wished they could come play Rock Band.

"When you let go of it," Henley said about the lantern, "you let your problems go, too." He lit the candle while I held the paper globe lightly, so as not to crush the thin paper.

But it turned out, I held it too lightly. The lantern wiggled right out of my hands, and I reached up into the sky to grab it, and Henley jumped to get it too, and our heads smacked into each other's as the lantern sailed away from us.

Henley rubbed his forehead.

"Oh my gosh! Are you okay?" I covered my mouth. I had lost the lantern and headbutted my . . . boyfriend?

The whole thing could have been so awkward—the most romantic moment of my life turned potential brain injury.

But it wasn't.

Because Henley started laughing.

And I started laughing, too.

"Do you want to come to my house sometime?" I asked him, and he said, "Definitely."

We stood on the deck, his arms around me, both of us breathing in O'ahu's salt, the sweet plumeria, the earth and ferns, the blue shadow of the mountains.

And time stretched out in front of us, over the 'āina, across the ocean.

SPRING

Prompt: "The clearest way into the Universe is through a forest wilderness." (John Muir, 1838–1914)

I was happy.

And I was happy that I was happy.

Even the shower water felt different. This morning, it was warm at first. But I wanted more than that. So I cranked the faucet to cold and stood under the water till I froze in my bones. Then I switched it back to hot, and my skin got all prickly, and I stayed there like that till I couldn't stand the hot anymore, and I made it cold again.

And like I did at the map in the mall, I wanted to laugh, and I even kind of did.

What was I laughing at? What was funny?

For a while, I turned the water up and down, forward and back, hot and cold, the prickle, then freeze, then burn, then prickle.

Then I opened the window wide, breathed in the Mānoa air, the mana ʻāina—the strength of the land—and I suddenly longed for the boldest Kona coffee, the kind you can only get from Glazers.

And the towel I took off the rack and pressed into my face was the softest thing in the universe. The palm fronds swished in the wind behind me, and the stained glass bird Mom and I bought last summer from the farmer's market caught the rising sun in just a way to show off the brightest blues and reds I'd ever known.

Here in language arts, I'm wide awake, and the Hawaii sun washes the mangoes from green to gold, turns the banana flowers purple, warms the Waikiki water. But me, I'm thinking about snow.

When I was four, or maybe only three, I got a pink bike for Christmas. It had white tires and white training wheels and flashy pink ribbons coming out of the handle bars. Now that I think about it, it was probably really low to the ground. But back then, it seemed really high up.

I was too scared to ride it.

I don't remember all the things Mom and Dad said or did to get me to try. I just remember I wouldn't go for anything.

Eli got on my pink bike, and his long legs pedaled up and down the street in front of me, the sparkly streamers whipping his knuckles as he called out, "See, it's easy!"

"I can't," I told him. "I'm scared I'll fall."

But Eli said he'd hold on to me the whole time, that he wouldn't let go. He looked so big, so tall, so strong. He seemed so sure.

For a long, long time on Christmas Day, I rode around and around in Oregon. It was snowing, but the snow wasn't sticking.

And Eli was holding me up.

SPRING

Prompt: "You, with your words like knives, and swords and weapons that you use against me." (Taylor Swift, "Mean")

"You'll never get past this."

Words like knives.

Tears are words.

"How will you ever get over what your brother did?"

This whole time, I've been asking myself the wrong questions. I've been wondering how Brielle could have said that to me. How she could be so mean, how she could wreck my life like that. I've been asking myself the same question Brielle asked me, how I'll get over what Eli did.

But what really matters is why it all got to me.

Swords and weapons that you use against me.

Anyone would think the worst day of my life was December 23. The day Koa and Tate died. The day Eli drove them off the highway.

One second, we were all dancing around the fire at Pipeline, and the next, there were tire tracks across Kamehameha and empty desks in English 12.

Dad got the call from Wahiawa General that Eli and I were in the ER, that Eli was being charged with all that stuff, that Koa and Tate were gone forever. He picked me up. I didn't need stitches. They said the cut on my eyebrow would heal on its own—it would just take time. But Eli didn't get to come home.

Until then, I had been practicing Beethoven's Sonata No. 25 every day. It was hard—two hands, timing, tempo—and I was getting really good.

But that day was the day I stopped. Mom's legs gave out right from under her in the kitchen when Dad told her. I helped him get her into bed, where she's stayed for the past three months, except when she went into the place with the courtyard and the koi, and the one day she made banana pancakes, and all of a sudden, Dad had a thousand department meetings and budget committees and curriculum development and changed his office hours to dinnertime.

Or you would think the day after, when Eli was charged, was pretty awful, too, when Mom first got in bed. Or the day Dad sent her away to the koi place. Or when my best friend turned on me, then said I wasn't making my life happen. That was all absolutely horrible. Terrible. Awful.

But there was one day that was worse than all those, even. One person who could have completely ruined my life.

SPRING

Prompt: Which modern invention could you not live without?

It's been three months and sixteen days since Dad pulled up by the flagpole the first day back from winter break.

"Please," I had begged him, my knees knocking against each other, "I can't. I'm sick. I'm going to throw up."

Earlier that morning, I kept falling back asleep, and Dad kept coming in to wake me up. Finally, he pulled off my covers and piled them on the floor and said, "Get up."

"Get up." Like that.

And still, I lay there, curled into myself. There was no way I could go back to school and see all those people. Everyone would judge me, label me, hate me. They would think I killed Koa and Tate. They would say things. They would talk about me. They would make stuff up and spread it around.

But Dad said, "It is time to go NOW."

What was I wearing that first day back? How did we get to the flagpole? I don't remember getting in the car, or driving with Dad.

"My stomach . . ." I tried to tell him.

He reached across and opened my door. "You'll just have to get through it," he said.

Somehow I got out of the car. I didn't go over to Li Lu's locker, and she didn't come to mine, like we had done every day forever. We didn't swap notes or playlists, or tell each other what happened between last night after we went to sleep and right when we were standing there at our lockers. We didn't talk about going to my house or her house after school, or the new Topshop shoes Brielle had, or how the guy Li Lu liked told her "Hey," or that Palakiku Kama was the one who had been stealing everything out of everyone's lockers, or that someone and someone had made out or broken up.

Somehow, when Dad left, I didn't walk back out the door. Maybe deep inside, I knew there was nowhere else to go.

I floated through the halls like my feet weren't touching the ground. Like a ghost.

"See!" I would have yelled to everyone if ghosts could talk. "YOU have nothing to worry about! I'M the biggest failure at this school! I have the worst life ever! My life is way worse than yours! My problems are SO MUCH bigger. Your life could be as bad as mine, but it's not, so you can feel good about that!"

Everyone was staring and whispering and pointing. They said I was the one who was driving. They said I was just as wasted as Eli. They said I covered for him with the Five-0. That he got sent off to military school. That the alcohol in his blood was double the legal limit. That this was his third or fourth DUI.

People said they always thought he was a loser. That he never cared about anything but surfing, that he wasn't that good anyway.

Sister Anne pulled me into her office first thing to "check in." She tried to force me to go to Grief Group, with people like Sachi Manhaloa, whose sister died from leukemia, and Olivia Huang, whose cousin drowned right at Sandys, and Ellie Williams, whose brother was killed in Afghanistan. But I couldn't go to Grief Group. With all the people who were there because of what happened at Pipeline. Because of what Eli did.

The teachers tried to act normal. They pretended like everything was the same as before.

Accidentally, I went to Latin instead of math, and I didn't realize it until Tae-sung told me to get out of his seat.

I wanted the day to be over so I could go back home. To shut myself in my room and close my eyes and sleep forever, like Mom. To wait it out, till it was over.

Nothing made sense.

After eighty minutes of threes and fives and other hieroglyphics, the bell rang, and math ended—just like that.

The day was somehow going on.

Latin made no sense. My body was getting bigger and bigger. I was pretty sure I was spilling all out of my seat, like dough rising all over the place. Everyone could see how much space I was taking up. I was enormous. I was everywhere. People tucked their arms into their sides and pulled their feet under their desks so I wouldn't pull them into my gross, doughy, sticky mess.

I tried to keep my arms by my sides and my feet under my desk, too.

At lunch, I stayed in the bathroom and cried until my eyes were bright red. It smelled like hot pee in there, and bleach, but I stayed in that last stall, so furious that Eli was still in bed, at home, asleep, while I was forced to be in the worst place on earth, because the rehab place Dad was sending him to in Montana couldn't take him for another few days. He'd had court. He'd been in jail. He didn't have to deal with any of this.

After lunch, I went to language arts. I didn't think it could possibly get any worse.

But it did.

SPRING

Prompt: "Don't run, stop holding your tongue."
(Sarah Bareilles, "Brave")

"Are you okay?" Miss Wilson asked.

The prompt was right there on the board, like it had been every day since September. I could see it, but the letters and words didn't mean anything, didn't make any sense. At first, I thought I could copy those letters and words. The pen weighed a thousand pounds. Somehow, I pushed it into the paper, dragged it down, got the first part. I tried to concentrate, studied the letters, the parts to them, arcs, circles, spaces, lines, the three dots that followed. I stared at the words.

"Prompt: On my mind is . . ."

On my mind is.

Is.

There was so much emptiness after.

On my mind is.

On my mind is . . . ?

Then Brielle turned around and said what she said.

"How will you ever get over what your brother did?"

And when I sat there, frozen, stunned, Brielle answered for me. "How is he still alive? He should be dead. You'll never get past this."

And after, I couldn't write anything. I couldn't think or talk.

Somehow that day, the rest of class happened, and the rest of school happened, too, and after school, I walked home. I took the avocado path. Usually, it took 39 minutes. But that day, it took 188. Or maybe it was five. Macario was right about time. It's immeasurable.

All day, I checked my phone to see if anyone had texted. Maybe they couldn't talk to me face-to-face at school, which I could understand, but maybe we were still friends, secretly. That would be okay.

But there were no texts from anyone. No missed calls. Nothing, even, from Li Lu. She hadn't texted or called or IMed me once since that fight we'd had about Brielle.

While I walked home, the rumors swelled. That I walked into Latin instead of math because I had come to school wasted, just like my brother always did, that I got high in the bathroom at lunch—"You should have seen how red her eyes were"—that I just sat there in language arts so baked, I couldn't even write the prompt.

People had a lot to talk about. The more they talked about me, the less other people would talk about them.

I was by myself in the rain on the avocado path, and at the same time, I was in the middle of it all, of the biggest drama ever in the history of Our Lady of Redemption. There was no way out of it, no getting through it. I had no future.

I hated my life. I hated myself.

Brielle was right, what she said that day. Eli, my brother, he ruined everyone's lives. He sent Mom away and took all my friends and cost us all our money and erased Koa and Tate.

Eli should have died. Why didn't he?

Why does he get to keep on living when everyone else is gone?

I hated him, my brother, who covered for me when I sent Hopper off to the wild pigs. I hated Eli and have known it since the day he came home and drank out of the faucet. I hated him. I had believed Brielle. That I'd never, ever, ever get past it.

SPRING

Prompt: Without looking back, what do you remember about the national tragedy from December?

A don't-look-back.

This is new.

But as much as I want to remember, I can't.

Why can't I?

I know it must be really important. But December seems like such a long time ago. A billion things have happened between then and now, between Pipeline and this, between Brielle and me, and me and Li Lu. There's been Eli's stuff, and Mom's stuff. And Dad. And math.

I want to remember three months ago.

But I can't. I've sat here and thought for a long, long time.

So has Henley. And Isabelle, and Tae-sung, and Brielle. No one knows. We're all sitting here trying to look back, and none of us can—none of us are writing—and Miss Wilson seems really sad about that.

FALL

Prompt: Respond to this morning's school shooting.

It's horrible.

We were watching it right as it was happening, on CNN in Mr. Montalvo's class—lines of students being herded out of classrooms, parents waiting to see if their kids were alive, pictures of people calling 911, tears, teachers, stretchers, hugs.

It's the day before winter break, and so many kids are just . . . gone.

We'll never get over it. We'll never forget.

He was all wrong, that boy, he shot his own mom. There was a picture of him, really bad hair and skeleton eyes.

What was he trying to show people? That he was fed up? That he was alone?

We're all fed up. We're all alone.

He hated everyone? He couldn't keep going?

We're ALL trying to make it. He did it to himself, cutting himself off. Hiding in his room.

He could have reached out to someone. He could have gotten help.

Why didn't somebody notice before it happened? There had to have been signs. I mean, who let him have those guns? Plus, he was

ALL OVER social media. PUBLIC forums. His parents, his grandparents, his group, teachers, hoalaunas—somebody must've known SOMETHING. Pay attention, people. LOOK AT WHAT'S RIGHT IN FRONT OF YOUR FACE!!!!

Now, it's everywhere. If that boy was looking for someone to notice that he was fed up, that he was alone, that he didn't fit in, that he wasn't making it, well, now the whole world has noticed. It's on CNN and Fox and ABC and CBS and MSNBC, and it will be on *Nightly News* tonight, and even *People.com*. It will be here, on O'ahu, on KHON2—instead of the flooding, the caved-in roofs, the mold and holes and uprooted trees, the delayed flights and rerouted streets.

Even here at OLR, we had a lockdown drill during second period just because of that boy super far away. Sister Anne's voice came on over the loudspeaker, saying staff is available in the counseling office. We were reminded to report anyone without a uniform or a name badge. There's a security guard, one with a hunched back.

Is it just me, or is it all of us who thinks this kind of thing is happening more and more?

That the darkest days of our lives are all stacking up on top of each other.

SPRING

Prompt: Imua!
("Forward")—King Kamehameha I

How have those families moved forward?

It's been three months and seventeen days since the shooting.

How have the sisters lived their lives without their brothers? How have the parents kept on living without their kids? How have the ones who were left behind, how have they moved forward?

Maybe time just went on. Maybe one day turned into another day, and that day turned into another, until the days turned into a month, and a month turned into three.

Maybe doing something good pushed them through. They started groups and movements and triathlons and charities. They organized school safety plans, tried to change laws, and aired PSAs. They worked. They fought so the ones they had lost wouldn't disappear forever.

I'm doing it, too. I'm fighting. The blueberries, I think they're finally kicking in.

This morning, before there was any light, the rooster up the road started crowing. And I woke up, and heard while the mynah birds woke up, too. Then from rooftops all around, doves started cooing. It was a chorus of birds, singing together. The sky lightened, and the first shades of red melted the mist over the Mānoa mountaintops, filling my eyes, all my insides, with that light, that glow, that promise that only morning can bring.

I am . . . awake.

I am healing, but I am hurt.

I am hurt, but I am healing.

SPRING

Prompt: "Once you know . . . you can't unknow . . . It's a burden that can never be given away." (Alice Hoffman,* Incantation*)

I wrote it all down, exactly how it happened. I hated my brother. I couldn't get how he was still alive. I would never move forward. I would stay stuck forever. I thought I deserved to. Li Lu was right.

Dad said he had put in an application back on the mainland, and I asked him where on the mainland, and he told me New Mexico, and I asked him why there, and he said maybe it would be good for us all to dry out in the desert for a while.

"We already tried the desert," I told him. Arizona. The desert didn't work, because we just moved on to Oregon.

"All of us? Mom, too?" I asked him. And he said, "Of course Mom, too."

"What about Eli?" I asked.

And Dad said he just didn't know about what was going to happen to Eli, and he didn't know if he would even get the job, or if he did get the job, if he would take it. He's just thinking about it, he said.

"But we might just leave him here?" I asked. "We'd leave Eli here, alone? By himself?"

Why do I care about leaving Eli behind? He didn't care when he changed our lives forever.

"How much percent?" I asked Dad, "One hundred? Or more like ten?"

Dad thought for a second: "Thirty," he said.

I watched him drive away along the monkeypods. Mom loved them so much. They were like giant umbrellas, trying to protect us in Mānoa.

Way down the hill, Honolulu stood up tall under the sun. It looked clean and quiet and calm from far away. If we move to the desert, we won't have monkeypods or hibiscus or plumeria. We won't have Waikiki, or Sandys, or Sunset, or Ala Moana. I'll get a new school, like I begged Dad for before, only now I don't know if I want that. I'll leave Henley behind. And I'll never meet anyone else like him. But leaving Eli, we just couldn't.

SPRING

Prompt: What's in your pocket?

It's all over. Just like that.

After three months and twenty-seven days, after that night that changed everything forever, no one is looking at me with blame and hate. They aren't whispering to each other in the halls about me, or pointing at me at lunch. They aren't judging my life anymore.

It's like it never happened at all, like Eli never drove Koa and Tate back from Ehukai, like he never rolled Koa's Jeep off Kamehameha into the pineapple plants, and crushed his best friends, and is in jail because of it.

All of a sudden, all people are talking about is Brielle, who isn't here today and, now that I think about it, wasn't here yesterday, either.

Already, the *Honolulu Star-Advertiser*'s plastered Brielle's dad all over the front page. And over and over, the KHON2 morning news has showed him being hauled out of their mansion in Kahala for tax fraud or something.

It's everywhere—Brielle's mom, hiding her face with big sunglasses and a hat, hustling out of her lawyer's office on Kahala Avenue.

The cheerleaders, the sand volleyball girls, the emo group, even—everyone is talking all about it.

But they're not talking about me.

People move on.

The thing that really wrecked me is the thing that saved me, too.

SPRING

Prompt: No Child Left Behind.

Brielle is back.

People are saying, "Oh my god" and "She looks HORRIBLE" and "They've lost EVERYTHING" and "Her whole life was fake."

Someone who lives way over in 'Ewa was saying she saw Five-0 tape all around the Bransons' iron gate, and all kinds of cop cars, and IRS SUVs, even. And that doesn't make any sense, because how would she know from the other side of the island? And someone else said, "There goes her mom's BMW, for sure."

Somehow, over just a couple days, Brielle had lost a lot of her usual tan. Like Eli did when he came home from rehab. But her hair was still brushed, and her suede shoes were brushed, and her shirt was ironed, and her socks were still pure white.

I couldn't forget how, in the beginning, when Eli's accident first happened and Dad made me come back to school, my hair was brushed, too, and my shirt was ironed, and my socks were pure white. In the beginning, you try to pretend that everything's still normal. You can pull it off for a while.

But me, I saw them—the black half-moons hanging under her eyes.

SPRING

Prompt: Karma.

"I'm not going," I told Dad this morning. "I'm staying here, with Mom and the dirt. You can't make us leave Eli."

Dad stared at me. "What?" He stopped stirring his coffee.

"I'm not moving," I said. "I'm staying here. I'm not starting over. I'm not like you."

I felt strong. Free.

Maybe Henley's family would have us, if we couldn't keep the house. I could get a job like Fetua. And Mom could help Nisha grow lettuce and lilliko'i.

"I'll have some of that coffee, too," I told Dad.

He slid over the pot.

Things were already different. Better. Maybe someday I'd get it, the Beckham tote. Stacy said she'd help me. I just wasn't sure I wanted it anymore.

"Hey!" Soo called out across the hall before class. "What's your number again?"

She said she'd accidentally deleted it from her phone, and did I want to have lunch tomorrow?

And I told her thanks, but I've been eating with Henley and Ryan Ling, who knows all about the Beatles and draws choose-your-own-adventure graphic novels. And Li Lu's been sitting with us, too. She gave me her almond cookie.

Soo sat in the courtyard right in Brielle's old place, with Puakea in Soo's old spot. And Brielle sat by herself with an unopened green tea smoothie, and I wondered how that was for her.

I did give Soo my number, though. She'll IM and PM and text me "hey" and heart emojis, and I'll have hers and tons of other friend requests when I log back into Facebook for the first time in forever.

It's not all perfect. My arms still feel longer than they really are, and Mom is under her quilt again, and Eli's in the O'ahu Community Correctional Center. The bills keep piling up on the counter near the fruit bowl, and desks rest empty in the back of English 12.

If the omamori works, maybe I'll pass math, or at least sleep a whole night without bolting awake from dreaming of the Jeep rolling over and over.

But today, after school, I'm going to Li Lu's house. She asked if I wanted to catch up on *Gossip Girl*, but I asked if we could actually do our math instead. First, we'll fight. I'll tell her, "Brielle Branson? You always HATED her. I was already DYING, and that whole thing WRECKED me."

And she'll bring up all the things I had written about her in my notebook.

Then I'll be sorry, and she'll be sorry, and we'll put on the "Friends" and "Forever" lockets we'd told each other we'd gotten rid of but really hadn't. We'll pick up our dreams right where we left off—deciding to sign up for the sunrise or sunset horseback riding session at Camp Mokule`ia, getting coconut lime pie at Buzz's after graduation. We'll sneak off to Waikiki and take pictures of tourists when they're not looking and laugh when we show each other, and get $10 manis at Paul Mitchell. Then we'll start high school. Finally. She'll take Mandarin, but I'll take French, and we'll make matching vases in ceramics. We'll get back into hula, and we'll tell each other everything. We'll act like it's the way it's always been, and maybe someday it actually will be.

But for Brielle, it was all just starting.

I saw her.

Standing in front of the locker-room mirror, a T-shirt and polo under the school sweatshirt nobody ever wears. And the skirt, its pleats hanging hopelessly soggy and sad.

She didn't see me at the other end by the sinks, tossing a tissue into the trash can on top of a ripped-open box of Diurex Ultras. Water pills. She was too obsessed with herself in the mirror by the benches, her sweatshirt pulled up with one hand while she pinched some skin at her waist with the other, mascara tears rolling down her cheeks.

SPRING

Prompt:

It's the Detention Convention. He's subbing.

"Yo, watch out . . ." Koa had told me.

Miss Wilson is sick, the Detention Convention told us. She was too sick, even, to leave plans for class. There's not even a prompt. He said we'd start by pairing up and sharing what we'd written in our notebooks about yesterday's prompt.

Miss Wilson would NEVER make us share! She always said our words are private!

And Henley, the ONE person I would share my words with, is gone watching Orchid's class play.

First and most importantly, I told myself, I am definitely NOT going back to detention. To that room with no posters and no plants, with the rigged clock and the slice of window. There was no way I was going to sit for sixty whole minutes again before the first bell rang and do absolutely nothing with all the ice heads.

So I looked to Isabelle, then to Hannah, but Isabelle was already pushing her desk over to Hannah. Amelia had paired up with Liam. Even Tae-sung had a partner.

In front of me, Brielle wasn't moving at all.

The Detention Convention came over, the pink pad in his hand,

and said, "Harper and Branson, is there a reason you aren't working together?"

Neither Brielle nor I said anything back. There were a billion reasons the two of us weren't working together.

He held out the pink pad so we could see it. "Well, if there's no reason, let's get to work."

Slapping the pad against his thigh, he walked to the front of the room and glared at us from there.

I flipped my notebook to yesterday's prompt. Still, the Detention Convention was up there glaring.

Almost painfully, like she had a broken back or neck or something, Brielle turned around. Her notebook rested on her knees—lines and lines and lines of nothing.

She looked up, and though I expected her eyes to be as empty as her notebook, they were filled up instead with a thousand arms reaching out.

Her heart, it was barely pumping.

It was everything I thought I'd hoped for. For Brielle to hurt as badly as I had because of her. It was all right in front of me, what I thought I had wanted so much, even more—KHON2's picture of the Brazilian bikini model who'd had Mr. Branson's baby on December 10. The night before Brielle Cut me. The last day Brielle posted that random quote on Facebook.

That was the real reason there was no Carnivale. Because things were completely unraveling. Brielle was never in Australia. She made up that rumor herself and was probably just home, in her house, suffocating, waiting for the trade winds to breathe life back into her.

I never thought it would go this far—with the cheerleaders whispering about how her mom stayed out partying till three in the morning, even on Tuesdays, with football players from the college. People Brielle never talked to are saying the pineapple people kicked Mrs. Branson out of the `Ohana for paying off the bikini model to keep the baby a secret, and that she and Brielle moved into an apartment in `Aiea, where they slept on mattresses on the floor. People said that Sophia had her acceptance taken away from USC and was couch surfing with friends and had gotten gonorrhea. Some of it was probably true, and a lot of it was made up, but all of it would feel the same to Brielle.

Brielle was dying. Part by part. Cell by cell. Even a pinprick would be the very end of her. All I'd have to do was something tiny, invisible, passive-aggressive. Like tell her that her khakis seemed kind of tight, ask her if they were Sophia's.

The Detention Convention loomed over Tae-sung, then cast a This-Is-Your-Last-Chance glance at Brielle and me.

"I can't go back there," Brielle rasped, the thousand arms reaching out from her eyes. "To detention. I can't."

I remembered that day in January when Brielle bragged to Isabelle about how fun detention was. I wanted to make myself believe that she was two-faced, a liar, that she should be sent back to detention. I remembered her telling me about Chance Cameron's chapped lips and the lifeguard stand at Sandys.

"I can't," Brielle said again.

The air between us was thick—gardenia, wood, and lily.

I mumbled, "Karma . . ."

What was I doing?

"Karma . . ." I said again, super slow. Was I really doing this? Helping her after she lied to me, stabbed me in the back, used me, said Eli should have died, told me I'd never move forward.

The Detention Convention was still watching. Isabelle and Hannah were chatting away. So were Amelia and Liam, Tae-sung and Evan.

Brielle rubbed the notebook's spiral between her fingers, nails chewed down, cuticles rough.

I couldn't help remembering being in Sister Anne's office, smoothing my skirt pleats, my own nails red and raw.

The hard thing is the right thing, I heard Mom say from far away.

And Dad: *There are people who get through things, and people who give up.*

What if Brielle couldn't get through? What if she couldn't save herself? Or what if she gave up, and I was the last person on Earth who could have done something about that?

"I wrote . . ." I said, ". . . about *Gossip Girl* . . . and getting manis . . . and high school next year."

"I can't," Brielle said in a small voice, not even really to me. Staring at the blank page on her knees, she said to no one, "My life . . . is over."

"Free time now, folks!" the Detention Convention yelled out from the front. "We can either write in our notebooks, or there's a nice stack of vocabulary worksheets up here."

I thought I'd be relieved to move forward from this enormously awkward situation with Brielle. To move onto anything but vocab. Brielle and me, if we had one thing in common, it's that we had both done the maximum amount of vocab worksheets a person could do in a lifetime.

Brielle's eyes were heavy. She was so tired.

You can't unknow. I thought about how writing had helped me since winter break. How my notebook was here when no one else was.

"Could you . . ." I started. For some reason, it flashed in my brain, that one day in September when Brielle crammed her notebook pages with capital *I*s, with letters that didn't touch each other at all, standing separately, apart, each alone. "Could you maybe . . . just . . . make a list?" I asked her.

Brielle blinked, like she saw me sitting there for the first time. "What do you mean?"

For a second, I wished I could take it back, that I hadn't said anything. I was backstabbing my own self. I had promised myself I'd never get over how Brielle said my brother should have died, how she brought my family into it and stole my best friend and my notebook and used me and Cut me. I swore I'd never get over how she labeled me and lipsticked my locker and erased me and wrecked my whole life.

And there I was, giving her a lifeline.

This whole thing wasn't playing out at all like I thought it would, where I watched Brielle hurt like I had.

I could hate myself for talking to her. Outside, the hibiscus blooms and drops and blooms again, like it always has. But something is different. Something has changed.

"Just a list," I said. "Of anything, of . . . like . . . the things right in this room, even?"

"A list . . ." Brielle said. Her face became a little more . . . awake. She picked up her pen, turned back toward the front.

Her wrist moves as she looks up at the clock, around the walls, out the window, her words curling into columns.

SPRING

Prompt: Look back.

My eyes sting.

The courthouse on Alakea doesn't look different now. It doesn't look different from most of the other buildings in Honolulu—a big gray box with tinted windows, banyan trees outside. It could be a bank, or offices, or even a department at UH. But it's the criminal courthouse. Murderers and robbers and ice heads are inside.

The room is brown. Brown walls, brown desks, brown benches where people wait like they're in church for their sins to be confessed.

I sneak in and sit in the very back. If I see it for myself, then I'll know the truth. People can say whatever they'll say, but I won't wonder what's real.

A reporter from KHON2 has a yellow notepad.

Dad sits near the front behind Koa's parents. Last night Mom's arms were around him. They were standing by their bedroom window. "I will bring you back from this," he said, his words on her forehead. He said he brought her back once, he'd bring her back again. I hope they don't see him. I hope they don't see me. Tate's mom isn't here. None of the surfers are here. I know Eli told them not to come. And they respected that.

Eli walks in the front. He doesn't look at any of us. He looks at the brown floor and sits at the brown desk. He is: splotchy temples, blazer borrowed from Dad, two sizes too big, all wrong with that tie. I would've picked him out something teal, maybe. To balance out all this brown.

A lot of talking happens. Laws, codes, numbers, dates.

The prosecutor is: Nude flats, navy suit. She has long hair and curves, and asks a lot of questions, but she isn't mean. She doesn't hate him. She acts like it's normal Eli killed two people.

And Eli answers the questions like it's normal he killed two people, too, like he practiced or something: "Kamehameha Highway," "45," "1:15," "a chicken," "swerved," "overcorrected," "swerved again . . ."

Then Eli's lawyer asks a lot of questions.

There's this: "Mr. Harper, can you tell the court why you were driving Mr. Okoto's vehicle on the night of the incident?" And Eli doesn't answer. He hasn't answered Dad the five thousand times Dad's asked it. Or the time I did.

I scoot forward.

The lawyer goes on extra slow: "Mr. Harper, was there any other means available to you than driving Mr. Okoto's vehicle?"

Eli shook his head.

"You couldn't sleep it off in the parking lot? Call someone? Take Uber, call a cab?"

"I couldn't think straight," Eli says. "I was . . . worried."

"You were worried about Mr. Okoto?"

"Objection," the prosecutor says.

Koa's lawyer clarifies, "Were you driving the vehicle because Mr. Okoto was under the influence of alcohol and methamphetamines?"

ICE?!?! Koa was an ice head? Impossible.

A whisper whips through the room.

Koa's mom buries her head into her husband and sobs. Did they already know about it? Eli looks at Dad for a split second, before looking away again.

"Is it true, Mr. Harper," the lawyer says, "that you were worried about the state of Mr. Okoto's health? That he was acting confused? That he told you something was wrong with his heart?"

There's silence.

What was wrong with Koa's heart? Why isn't Eli answering the questions? How does the lawyer have all this information? Why don't I know any of this? Why didn't Eli tell me?

"You didn't call 9-1-1? Or go to the Sunset Beach Station right there? Or call Mr. Okoto's parents?"

Eli takes a slow breath, closes his eyes. He answers, "Koa was out of chances."

The lawyer walks up close to Eli. She speaks kindly, right to him. "Mr. Harper, did you drive Mr. Okoto's vehicle the night of December 15, to avoid your friend getting into any more trouble? . . . Because he had told you if he 'crossed the line' once more, his parents would send him to military school in Virginia?"

Eli does not look at the Okotos.

The lawyer turns to the audience. "Can you confirm, Mr. Harper, that Mr. Okoto was terrified of going to military school? That he was terrified to leave O'ahu, the ocean, his school, his friends? He had a future, correct, as a semiprofessional surfer? And he had a girlfriend?"

"Mr. Harper . . ." The lawyer turns back to Eli. "Please tell the court your motivation for driving Mr. Okoto's vehicle at one a.m. on December 15 from Ehukai Beach Park down Kamehameha Highway."

Eli's eyes narrow. His head shakes slightly. He won't say, I know he won't. He won't give the reason he was driving Koa's Jeep, I think. He hasn't yet, and he never will. What went down went down, but it happened in the surfing world, so the rest of us will never know.

"Mr. Harper?" the lawyer prods.

My god, my god, my god, my god.

Eli.

The lawyer walks over to Eli, but he turns and faces the rest of us.

"Is it because, Mr. Harper, on the night of December 15 you didn't want to hurt your friend? Instead, you were trying to protect him?"

It was like the Hopper situation that night at dinner.

Eli the superhero. Strong, superhuman, defender of the weak. He would never tell why he was driving Koa's Jeep.

For the first time in the trial, Eli looks at me. Eli the manslaughter defendant in Hawaii criminal court. His jaw sags like his jacket. His shoulders sag. All his bones turn to sand.

And then Eli presses his palms into the sockets of his eyes, and the tips of his fingers dig into his scalp. And he stays just like that.

What's he doing? He's never done that before. Is he hiding from us? From himself?

I want to run up there and pull his hands off his face. I want to punch him and scream.

But also, though, I want to hug him, to hold on to him.

I don't.

I don't do anything. I'm stuck on the brown bench, wondering why. Why is Eli doing that with his hands on his face?

And after some seconds or minutes or maybe hours, Eli is charged with second degree negligent homicide and sentenced to prison for three years, probation for two more, and Dad lets out a cry like a hurt animal in the darkest part of night. It's a gasp for air and a cry of pain all at once.

But Eli's palms stay pressed to his sockets till the Five-0 take him by each of his arms and lead him to a side room, and he starts his time away from us, from his friends, from school, from his future, from the water.

Me, I am sentenced to Our Lady of "Redemption" for four more years, two months, and eleven days. I sit in language arts with this notebook, writing it down, trying to get it, why it's wrecked me, Eli doing that with his hands.

Because I've never seen him do that before?

Because I didn't know why? Or what it meant?

Because he hates himself? Because he's not perfect? Because he screwed up?

No one is perfect. People screw up.

It is part of being human.

Eli's no crusader, but he's not a killer, either. He's a person, a brother, a son, a friend.

I know I will miss him. My life won't be the same. Mom's and Dad's lives won't be the same. Eli's life won't be the same.

But he is still here.

He is here.

Is it possible for me to be sad and mixed up and miss Koa and Tate, and at the same time be so glad about that?

SPRING

Prompt: On my mind is . . .

My hands scoop through the deep blue that's warmer than I thought it'd be, my thighs flat against the old Quintara. I'll see what this is all about.

The waves at Waikiki are always ankle biters. By now, almost summer again, they've died down to mush.

Koa would be laughing—low shorts, hair in his eyes.

"Get it, Grom!" Eli'd be laughing with him. They'd laugh and laugh into the sky.

Eli always wanted me to try.

It turns out he didn't want me to watch him do fancy drops from big waves. He wanted me to do it, to share it, to feel what he felt about the water. He wanted me to know.

I'll tell him. When I visit.

I'm bringing the note Tate's mom gave me to give to him. It says, "Eli, honey, Tate would want you to know it'll be okay."

She could forgive him. And if she could forgive him, maybe some of the rest of us could someday, too.

Me, I'll tell him I found it—the lucky cat bank I got from Chinatown. Right in the freezer, where he stuck it before he went away again.

* * *

The tiny waves plink against the bottom of the board, and I listen, let the water roll softly under me, raising me up and letting me down. I breathe in the sun, the salt, the sea, the wax.

Left hand then right, I paddle out again.

I'm not the next Carissa Moore.

I'm just a girl scooping through the water, my bag and the rest of the world farther and farther behind me.

Leash around my ankle, tying me to the board, I paddle out toward the sun.

I scoop with my left hand, then my right, then I scoop with both. My arms burn, so for a second, I stretch them out behind me. And I rest like that, the waves rocking me forward and back, my cheek on the board, eyes closed, fingertips dragging along in the water.

Tears are words

Waiting to be written.

On my mind is . . .

Keep writing!